The Misfortunes
of
Tommelise

(a Dark, Why Choose Thumbelina Retelling)

R.N. Arcadia

To those who enjoy a wintry choose fairytale retelling.

Authors Note

This is loosely based on the tale of Thumbelina, however, because it was a kid's story, all the characters are aged up to 21+. *And no beetles and jitterbugs.* Names and creatures, plus the setting were slightly changed to make the world more adult and darker. This retelling is a dark, why choose, and may not be suitable for all readers.

Some themes include, but are not limited to mentions of trafficking, drug use, Non-con/rape (not detailed), elements of BDSM, Stockholm Syndrome, taboo themes (there are three triplet witches, one soul split into 3—a grey area), a stabby fae, self-harm, bondage, hints of DD/lg, uses of dominance and submission, suicidal ideation/attempt, kidnapping (multiple times like in the original movie), violence…

If there are any TWs I missed, please know it was not my intention to mislead anyone.

Please note the elements of BDSM described in this story are not to be portrayed as real. Abuse is abuse and that is not how it really is, and this author does not support abuse or abused consent. No means no. Please, always research and practice safety when trying anything BDSM related.

If you read the Fairytales Reloaded Anthology from late fall 2023 (Down in Grimm's Dungeon) under the R.N.A. pen name, please skip ahead to Chapter 12 from where the anthology left off, or feel free to start from the beginning!

The Story So Far...

The city of Sirap, Ecnarf, is bright, bold, and bustling with a steady thrum of energy, an illusion to those unaware of the sinister empire that resides underneath. A city with no rules and a king who reigns in blood, terrorizing those who threaten to take what's his. The destitute live outside the city, at the mercy of the crime ring. The Supernatural lingers within the shadows, disguising themselves as light, as monsters do.

Though there is darkness, there is light and love to behold.

On the city's outskirts, a woman was plagued with sadness for she could not have children. The woman had heard tales of a powerful warlock who could bestow gifts to those seeking, for a price. Overcome with the hope of having a child, the woman summoned the warlock. She was willing to give anything he asked.

A soft rapping on her door startled the woman from her silent summoning; her heart began to thrum in her chest. Another rap, harder this time, had the woman moving from her small wooden table to open the door.

Outside stood a man shrouded in darkness; it was only a moment before a strong voice reverberated throughout the small cottage. "I've heard your wishes," he began as his voice slithered around the woman, "I only ask for one night with you, and you shall have your child."

The woman gasped at his request. A feeling of unease settled within as she remained silent, considering the warlock's price.

Finally, the woman agreed, desperate for a child.

Lo and behold, a beautiful baby girl was born nine months later, *Tommelise*. The bouncing bundle of joy brought her mother the happiness she longed for. Unfortunately, fate would not be so kind to Tommelise.

She stopped growing, leaving her to remain smaller than those around her.

During her adolescent years, Tommelise read many books about the fae who lived amongst her, their tales of supernatural lovers and mates becoming a fascination. Having grown up outside of the city with her mother and animals on the farm, she had no idea about such intimacy. But the older she became, the more she craved it.

Still, Tommelise spends her days singing and dancing, learning all she can from her mother's enriching library while dreaming of the day she could venture into the city and experience the neon lights sparkling in the distance. The city's glimmer gave rise to dreams, the bright lights beckoning her to its dark perfection. Fate awaited her there; she could feel it.

On the day of Tommelise's twenty-first birthday, she ventures into the city in search of dazzling dreams, hopeful of her storybook's promise. As the lights come into view, Tommelise wonders if the fae is anything like the stories, and if they are, is it possible that she could have mates too?

Tommelise takes a deep breath as she steps into the glow of the luminous lights, a smile dancing on her lips.

As she walks further into the city, a dark energy awakens, for the world is far too big and dangerous for such a tiny woman.

Chapter 1

"You're the One that I Want."

Tom

The neon lights couldn't prepare me for what lingered inside the city of Sirap, Ecnarf. The overcast sky looked as if it would open any minute. I began that day by getting my ID, courtesy of my mother, and some money to buy myself a present.

"Please, be careful, Tommelise. You do not know what monsters lurk in the city of bright lights."

I assured her I would be careful and return home safely. The dilemma I was faced with was, *what would I wear?*

My shoes met the pavement on the busy sidewalks. There were horns from vehicles, cursing, idle chatter, and *everything was so much louder.*

It was initially overwhelming, as the quiet farmhouse outside the city was all I knew.

The city made me feel little, *tiny even.* The dark gray buildings loomed in the sky, adding to the allure of the bustle and money that made the city thrive, no doubt.

People passed by me, shoving along in a curt way I wasn't used to. My height difference from everyone else made me feel out of place in such a big world. The noise of the city distracted me for a long while from finding the perfect outfit for my night out.

Between people-watching, shopping, and learning what all the different sounds of the city were, like the rushing sirens from police cars, and the sound of trains underground—I did manage to find a suitable outfit. A blue cocktail dress. It was modest but showed just enough skin, leaving room for the imagination should someone try to sweep me off my feet.

Doubtful, but possible.

Throughout the day, I began to find an odd charm in city life. My mother disagreed, which is why I spent over a month practically begging her to let me make this trip.

"I just want to see it once. I don't have to go back if I don't like it. I want to experience something new. Is that so wrong?" I had asked her while helping her cook one evening.

She sighed, giving me a look of defeat. "I left the city because of the chaotic nature and the crime. I worry for your safety. As your mother, I'm allowed to worry about my only child. But you are a woman, not a child, and I can't stop you."

I squealed in delight, hugging her tight as she stifled a laugh.

Smiling to myself over the memory, I saw some posters on a board in one of the shops while browsing for shoes to match my dress.

The Parisian: Karaoke Night.

Finding my evening plans, I eagerly browsed, noticing the sky darken outside the store.

After purchasing my shoes, I found somewhere to donate my old attire, tugging my coat tight around me. The checkout lady in the shop was nice enough to share where The

Parisian was and offered more information without me coaxing it out of her.

"It's the hottest nightclub in the city! You will have a blast and the best birthday!"

I gave her a glistening smile as I thanked her, finding food along the way to the place.

After eating, the city's luminosity nearly blinded me. The dull gray of the daytime didn't compare to how the city lights ignited the dark sky. There was a steady drizzle as I ambled along, taking in the gigantic buildings and lit signs everywhere in the heart of the city.

Somehow, I found myself standing under a red neon sign, *The Parisian.* The writing was elegant and fancy, and a line formed outside the entry behind me. Stepping inside, the crowd was ushered in after checking IDs and being stamped on the hand with a fancy *"P"* to show we were old enough to drink.

The city was alive, and its energy emanated my blood, fueling me forward. I gave my coat to the concierge, grabbing money for drinks.

Booming thumps pulsated through the walls before the double doors were pulled open, and I walked into a large open space with flashing lights and a crowd dancing near a booth where someone was creating music. I later found out that they're called a *DJ.*

Taking in the surroundings, it was mostly an open room, with a top floor above and stairs in the left corner, leading away somewhere. Overwhelmed, I made my way over to where drinks were being served at the bar.

While waiting there, I gave myself a quick mental pep talk. *You wanted a night out. You wanted to see what the city had to offer. Drink and dance, then find the karaoke. Have fun!*

Nodding at my thoughts as if someone else spoke them, a pretty woman came to me with a smile, asking what I wanted to drink.

"It's my birthday. What do you think I should try?" I spoke loudly so she could hear me, and her lips stretched farther as she pulled her long, dark hair into a high ponytail.

"I have just the thing," she stated before moving about and making whatever concoction it was.

The unfamiliar beats reverberated through my skin and ears. Although the beats were fast, they were melodic too.

Darker and sultrier. It was indeed a new experience, and I couldn't wait to make my way into the warm-bodied crowd.

The woman returned with a drink that looked like some sort of potion that faded from purple to pink, then a lambent blue.

I paid, stepping away before trying the suspicious-looking potion drink. Once the liquid met my tongue, my eyes rolled back. Whatever it was, it tasted like *magic* with how delicious it was. It was sour, then sweet, an exciting mixture that had me draining it dry and running up to get another before making my way to the dance floor.

I began to relax after the second one, my body tingling, and a feeling of euphoria enveloped me in the heat of the room *and the warmth of the crowd.*

The feeling of being watched prickled the back of my neck as I snaked my way through the crowd toward the center, the thrum of energy from the room making me nod my head and my body catch up to the unfamiliar rhythm.

I thought nothing of the feeling as I began to move. I was a tiny person in comparison to everyone around me, after all. Looks from the partygoers would be a natural happenstance.

The song changed minutes later, and I began to feel a slight lightheadedness that quickly dissipated into smiles and giggles. *So, this is what alcohol feels like, huh?*

I followed the crowd's body movements, mimicking some of the other women, while doing what felt right to me and the music. City life paved the way to a new dynamic that I wasn't used to, but it was intoxicating all the same. Funny how I was led here, to this moment. A dance club, drinking and dancing to my little heart's content. *A thing of dreams. This was exactly what I needed tonight.*

Elated over such a revelation, the surroundings around me began to blur. Finding it amusing, I happened to turn around, coming face-to-face with a handsome male. His dark red hair gave him a mysterious allure under the flashing lights with his all-black attire and a wicked, up-to-no-good smile on his face. *Oh my.*

The effects of the drinks drove me to be brave. I held out my hand to him in invitation as he watched me. His lips curled up as his eyes fixated solely on me. His energy was reeling me in as if I were a worm on a hook. When he took my hand in acceptance, he spun me around once before pulling me closer against the hard surface of his chest.

Feeling light and airy, I giggled over the intimate gesture, inhaling the scent of cedarwood and amber—*so titillating.* The man smelled amazing, and I couldn't help running my hands up his chest to his shoulders, catching the gaze of bright green eyes that reminded me of *home.*

Saying nothing and wondering what I smelled like to him, we moved *sensuously* against one another. *As if my body already knew how to move with his.* Those green eyes remained locked on mine with an added look of intent that I couldn't decipher. I turned around and leaned my head to the side as he placed a daring kiss in the crook of my exposed shoulder, settling his hands on my hips.

Who are you, Tommelise, and where is that shy, sheltered girl? The city has made you brazen.

My lips curled up at the thought. *It was my birthday, and it was time to finally live a little.*

His breath tickled me, causing my senses to zero in on where his body and mine touched. I hadn't realized how much I craved it until the man against me initiated it. The books I read were not enough to describe such a new sensation. It was riveting, and I couldn't wait to see where the rest of the night went. Dancing with him felt so *right.*

The handsome stranger could move the room with his looks, certainly towering over me—he exuded power and somehow chose *me* out of everyone to dance with. It was special, no matter his motive.

I closed my eyes, relishing his presence and how his body pressed against mine. His body heated me from the inside as we moved like we were molded into one, remaining like that for a few songs.

Eventually, I turned to face him, asking if he wanted to sing some karaoke. *How drunk I must sound to him.*

His husky laugh touched my ears, causing my cheeks to heat up. Not shying away, he took my hand and led me from the sweaty crowd.

The warmth from his hand made me feel giddy. I didn't care about his motives of possible ill-intent. I was along for the ride. *Would this be the start of a fling or something real?*

I could only learn so much from books without doing as the characters did. *Such naughty things, too.*

Thrilled by the prospect, I followed him up the stairs and down a long hallway that was bathed in red lighting. Another turn at the end opened to a large, cozy room with a completely different atmosphere than the party downstairs.

A group of women were singing off-key on stage to an unfamiliar song as the handsome stranger led me to a high-top table tucked in an intimate corner, away from the drunken people and terrible singing.

When he turned to me again, I introduced myself, "I'm Tommelise, by the way, but please call me Tom."

"You are fascinating, Tommelise; my name is Nelly." As he introduced himself, I felt his sultry voice reach deep, dark parts of me.

Nelly. An interesting name for the male that stood in front of me.

Giving him a shy look, his mouth lifted as he took the hand he held and placed a gentle kiss on top.

"It's lovely to meet you, *Nelly.*"

"The pleasure is mine, I assure you."

I gave him a cautious smile as he helped me into the chair, hands settling on my waist as he lifted me. Resisting the urge to clench my thighs at the gesture and how I enjoyed his touch, his eyes lingered on me before pulling away.

"I chose this place to celebrate my birthday today," I spoke without thinking, "for the dancing *and* the singing, but it looks like I need to show them how it's done."

I covered my mouth, realizing I sounded harsh. Nelly tilted his head, leaning back to laugh.

"I'll put your name in, Tom. We can even do a duet if you'd like."

My eyes lit up as I nodded excitedly while his laughter followed him. Fascinated by him, I watched him walk away, taking note of how glorious he looked in all black. His pants formed against his backside nicely, and I wondered what lay underneath. He was already dreamy. Was he equally so naked? *Would I find out?*

I shook my head at my thoughts. *You just met the guy, and you are already picturing him naked.*

Stuck in the internal battle until Nelly returned, I realized he had brought drinks with him.

Sitting next to me, he indicated his head toward the stage on the other side of the room, "There's a line ahead of us, so we might be here a while. I'd love to get to know you better. *Also, happy birthday."*

Beaming over his words, I thanked him as he picked up the two small glasses and handed me one, toasting *to me.*

"*Cheers to you, sweetheart, and what is sure to be an intriguing evening."*

I toasted with him and drank whatever was in the glass, nearly choking over the sting at the back of my throat.

Nelly stifled his laugh, rubbing my upper back. "You haven't drank alcohol like this before, have you?"

I shook my head as I caught my breath. Amusement danced on his handsome face, reaching his lips.

"Not until tonight," I admitted, trying not to stare at his lips. Instead, I found him looking at *mine.*

Thankfully, he distracted me first. "So, Tom, tell me more about you. What brings you to the city?"

Without thinking or sparing details of my quiet little life, I rambled on, explaining all about myself. I told him where I grew up, and how I wanted the first night in the city to be on my twenty-first birthday. And how I was a daydreaming farm girl.

Strangely enough, he listened to every word, gazing at me between sips of whatever we drank. He would chuckle where appropriate here and there, commenting, and asking questions about the animals on the farm. I quickly realized how comfortable I was with him, speaking as if we were two old friends. We were so engrossed in our conversation that I almost missed my name being called somewhere behind me.

Nelly and I locked eyes briefly before I got up, making my way over to the front. Nervousness overtook me as the host asked me to choose from a list. Having never done karaoke, the host told me to pick and follow the words on the screen. I nodded at them, selecting a song called *"Dangerous Woman" by Ariana Grande.*

As the music began, I stepped on the stage and found the screen displayed with words on it. *All I have to do is follow the words. I can do this!*

Finding some confidence and my passion for singing, I took a deep breath.

I followed the melody and words shown to me. *Here's to hoping I'm doing this right.*

It took a moment for my vocal cords to warm up, but after the first chorus, I felt more in my element and started to move with the words and microphone. The crowd began to cheer, and I wondered if Nelly was watching. I couldn't tell over the harsh stage lights unless people sat in the front two rows.

The song's lyrics were fitting for my evening out, so the applause that followed at the song's end made me proud. My first public song. I was a dangerous woman because I tasted freedom in the neon city.

I smiled at the crowd as the host repeated my name with Nelly's. I stood near the side as he chose a duet called *"You're the One That I Want."*

He met me with a cute, secretive smile as I followed him to the center of the stage, awkwardly waving to the crowd as the song started up.

It was completely different from what I just sang, but I followed his lead as he shot me a look and began to shimmy his shoulders, wiggle his hips to the beat, and sing out the lyrics.

Standing in shock, I almost missed my cue from the words on the screen.

My God, did he sound absolutely sexy, and those moves…

Nearly drooling over him, I began to sing my parts, mimicking his movements as we moved around the stage. The song was fun and different, and sharing it with Nelly was the peak of my evening out. His energy captivated not only me but the crowd, too.

Sadly, before I knew it, the song was over, and the crowd was cheering once more. We leaned into each other's side before leaving the stage to return to our table, hidden away.

"Not only are you insanely beautiful, *but you're talented, too,*" he told me, leaning closer. My breath caught in my throat at his proximity, seeing those handsome eyes move closer and closer until his lips met mine.

Chapter 2

"Fated to a Devil Like Me"

Chapter Playlist:
"Afterlife" by XYLO
"Castle" by Halsey
"Swan" by Willa
"THE DEATH OF PEACE OF MIND" by Bad Omens
"Bloodstream" by Transviolet

Nelly

I stood on the rooftop of the tallest building, the rough breeze blowing my dark red hair around my face as I watched below. The cars and lights, the rush of everyone being in a fucking hurry to get somewhere.

My city was my domain. To reign as I saw fit. I paved my way to the top in blood, my ruthless nature giving my enemies pause when they saw me *or tried to take from me*. Of course, I always showed them why *that was unwise*.

As the city worked its magic below, tricking everyone into never leaving, I remembered what it took to get to this point. The enemies that lay dead in the wake of my destruction and blood. I wasn't always like *this*. Hungry for blood as if it were my lifeline. *No*, it took losing everything to *gain* it. Sirap, Ecnarf wasn't my first home. I came from the Realm of the Fae.

There was a brutal war. It was so terrible that most of *my* kind died. My mother and father ruled in one of the kingdoms, and their mistakes eventually caught up to them. In their shame, for all of their wrongdoings, they cut off the tips of my ears to hide *our heritage.* I was led to believe there were no remaining family members.

In my grief, I slew my parents for their abuse and crimes after abandoning me in Sirap, Ecnarf. I could still smell the flames from their flesh as if it happened yesterday. I kept my mother's green necklace as a reminder of where I came from and all I had lost. The small green gemstone matched my eyes, and the chain was gold; I kept it hidden in my desk drawer, *out of sight and out of mind.* To deal with such unfortunate events in a new world alone, I cut off my magic, *the essence of me.*

Maybe the war changed my parents. However, *you don't abandon your fucking kid.*

I would rule differently, one that was wrought by my survival and coldness.

War taught me many things: how to kill a man, how to take, and how pretty crimson was as it spilled. I quickly discovered who was loyal.

Once word spread around the city of someone *new* claiming the territory over the city's center, enemies came from all sides. I discovered I wasn't the only fae from my world during my rise to power. Many who escaped war and survived were as lost as I once was. I built my foundation and returned their wills of survival.

One of the fae happened to be my cousin, which brought me strange relief that my family existed. Buz held no bitterness over what my parents had done in their rulings. He had his own vision of the future. I found out quickly how loyal he was after I slaughtered one of the families who killed his.

Usually, I didn't believe in killing our kind, but *family was everything.* I had so few already that I took matters into my own hands.

Buz and the rest of the fae that came out of the shadows cut off their fae ears to show loyalty. I asked him what he wanted and what would give him purpose.

Buz had requested, "Let me roam in the shadows. I'll do the spy and tech network for you. I lost everything, Nel. I don't want to rule; just let me aid in whatever you need. You are my blood and my chosen family."

I agreed, *you don't fuck with family,* and everything I set out to do took off from there. Between my rise of claiming the city's center and experimenting sexually with men, women, *and orgies,* Buz hadn't left my side since.

Family was created, not born. We don't choose what families we're born into; *we make them.*

We weren't taught any better, whether it was rules of relationships or loyalty versus family. *Thanks, Mom; thanks, Dad—oh wait, you're dead for being fucking terrible. Whoops.*

You left behind a vengeful son.

Closing my eyes and breathing the evening air brought me back to the present. It was a journey to get to where I was, and I wasn't alone. Fate always led to where I was meant to be.

My eyes opened slowly as I looked off into the distance, getting back in touch with my senses. The breeze, the sounds below, the echoing of my heartbeat, and the beauty around me from the city life. Something about that summer night called to me. It was in the air, a buzzing energy, a craving for something more.

Hopping down from the ledge of the building and making my way back inside, I decided to venture into the chaos and noise. Maybe fate would lead me somewhere, or a woman would finally catch my eye.

I struggled with relationships, and marriage wasn't something I was fond of. It seemed like a big commitment, and I couldn't have just anyone warming my bed *or owning my heart.*

Too many times I was fucked over by women who wanted my money or some sort of status in the city. *I sent them packing with the other dogs.* My time was too valuable to waste on temporary women. There was no rush for such frivolities. However, I wouldn't turn down an excellent opportunity to fuck should one arise.

I needed a queen to rule beside me. Not some gold-digging whore.

Wondering if such a person existed, I walked onto the slick streets and made my way toward my club, *The Parisian.* Upon entry, an electric buzz filled the air as the bass of the beats vibrated against my skin, lingering in my ears. Buz and a few of my guys leaned against the red-lit bar, drinking *The Garden Fairy,* mixed with absinthe and fresh, bold flavors. I shook my head in amusement as a whisky slid over the counter to me. Nodding my head at the bartender and my guys, I turned to observe the room around me.

The place was becoming busier, with the mingling bodies dancing salaciously. Buz leaned in my ear to remind me of a crime family causing disturbances in the city's outer rings. I rolled my eyes, feeling irritated when all I wanted to do was relax.

"Tomorrow, worry about it *tomorrow,*" I told him.

He nodded, finishing up his drink before leaving me there.

I did the same, wondering if I could find a woman to dance with. Despite my life's heartache and singleness, those earlier times did make me realize that I enjoyed both men and women. Women mostly came onto me, and the rival men wanted to kill me. I would settle for what I could get, but I doubt any male would approach me in my club.

Grabbing another whisky, I meandered over to the side, observing the dance floor. Initially, nothing really caught my attention or alerted me to possible threats. As the city's king, I always needed to be mindful of the world around me.

Bodies mingled together, grinding and nearly having sex on the dance floor; some were barely wearing anything. The flashing laser lights and strobes gave a tracer effect around the room. Finishing my drink, I did another look-over. Everything appeared normal until my eyes stopped on a woman in a blue cocktail dress.

My eyes traveled up to her tiny legs. *Who let this child in here?*

The girl was the shortest person in the crowd, but her natural long red hair caught my attention, and the way she swayed her hips. Caught in a trance, I finished my drink and made my way over. It began as mere curiosity.

Once I was upon her, I realized she wasn't a child at all, but the most beautiful woman I've ever seen with eyes so blue, my heart was captive. I forgot how to breathe as she held her hand to me, catching on to my intense stare. I took her hand without another thought, giving her a spin.

The woman before me stole all my thoughts and attention as we danced close, probably too close for her partially inebriated state. Nonetheless, I breathed her in as she turned in my arms.

Blackberry and vanilla orchid, sweet and enchanting, just as I gathered she would be. Something about her scent called to me as if it were a magic potion meant to bring me into her grasp.

I placed a kiss on the crook of her neck and noticed how her body reacted to my touch. Smirking and tucking the thought away for later, I realized she had no idea who she was dancing with. It was humbling how she knew nothing of the fae crime king at her back. *Otherwise, she'd run in the opposite direction.* Or towards my money. Although, perhaps I'd chase after her.

The beauty had curves in her tiny frame, and I only stood about a foot taller. *Perfect for resting my chin on top of her pretty little head.* She tucked under me nicely. I wondered how I would tuck into other places of hers, too.

The woman caught me off guard when she asked to do karaoke *instead of jumping my cock.*

I laughed, not knowing what else to do, but found her more endearing, nonetheless.

Over drinks, she told me all about her quiet life on the city's outskirts under the trees, along with the farm and her mother.

Tommelise. A strange and unusual name, but beautiful and unique, just like she is.

The more I learned about her, the more I realized how much I *liked* her. I hung onto her every word as she went on to tell me her life story.

This tiny woman was walking perfection, innocent, and naïve to the *little* world outside the city.

It made me want to protect her and keep her safe from the cruelties she would undoubtedly suffer if she kept coming to the city alone. I wanted to keep her alive and her hope, along with that cheerful demeanor. It was something people around me didn't have. *Myself included.*

Tom's name was called to the stage, pulling me out of my trance. We shared a look of that connection as she walked shyly on stage. I thought for sure she was out of her element until she opened her tiny mouth.

Tom's voice enraptured everyone in the room around her. *A dangerous woman, eh?*

I locked eyes with her from across the room, and I felt the pull of her all the way down to my cock. *Down, boy. Now's not the time for that, but soon.*

Tom couldn't see me from the blinding lights of the stage, but when she finished, I made my way over after both our names were called. I chose a song that I thought she would have fun singing and dancing to. *You're the One That I Want* started playing through the speakers as the words danced across the blue screen.

It felt like we belonged together. She was fun, and I hadn't remembered smiling so much before she came into my club. *Or laughing.* Laughter only came with my cohorts or during sex whenever I was buried deep inside them.

We finished our duet, leaning into one another before leaving the stage as cheers bounced off the room's walls. Back at our table and unable to resist any longer, I kissed her.

Those lips felt like coming back to life where there was none before. She gave my song meaning and light amidst my darkness.

As a child, I recalled reading an old book about the fae when I was roaming the castle library. It was a book about how to tell when one found their fated mate *or mates.* The book described how it could be multiple and of any species. It was as if I stumbled upon a secret, a key to unlocking the inner parts of my dark world. There was already chaos in the kingdom before war broke out, and I dove into those fairytales. My heart raced as I read about the telltale signs and *gifts of the fae,* as it read. *Visions and dreams. An irrevocability. Fate. Carnal cravings.* There were a few of them. It described a mate bond as an intense obsession, the need to protect and devour—sex sealed the bond.

The flashbacks flooded me as I remembered. It was no fairytale, and my mate was here in my arms.

Who knew that it would be Tom?

In disbelief over the revelation, I deepened the kiss and heard her moan.

I nearly fucking lost it with such a sound.

Holding her against me, I kissed her until we were breathless and panting. *Then, she bit her fucking lip.*

My thumb grazed her lip, pulling it down as she gave me a hazy-eyed look that made my cock strain against my zipper. *It's a good thing I was wearing all black and could hide my hardening length by how we were positioned at the table.*

"Do you want to stay here with these people singing off-key?" I asked huskily, trying to contain myself. "Or..." I paused long enough for her to lean closer and for me to whisper in her ear, "Can I tempt you with less noise and more of *me?*"

I pressed my nose into her neck before placing a gentle kiss there. An invitation to lure her further into my lair. To taste what lies between those thighs and under that blue dress.

I needed to have her in every way, but I'd settle for just a taste.

Mate or not, I couldn't give all of myself at once. We needed to trust each other even if my cells were on fire, signaling me to bend her over and fuck her.

Leaning back to catch her half-lidded eyes and biting her lip *again*, I knew my answer.

Tom wasn't as innocent as she appeared and seemed to ache for *my touch*. Her body told me all I needed to know. She leaned closer and gripped me tight in a way that made me fucking feral for more than a taste.

I wouldn't fuck her that night, even if I wanted to. Tom deserved more than me just being an animal, a*t least for now.*

I'd give her something better. A taste that would bring her back to me.

"Come with me," I murmured while taking her hand and leading her out of the room, down several hallways and stairs. My office was underground, hidden away from view. I entered the code on the door, a click sounding as the automatic warm-toned lights came on, giving an ambiance to the dark forest green office.

Her blue eyes were wild and glazed over; a rush of insanity hit me, and I could no longer keep myself from her. I pulled her into the room, shutting the door behind us.

I didn't give her time to admire my office with its dark oak furniture and the dark green walls with fun sconces creating a forest feel. I captured Tom's lips, pulling her toward me as I walked us to my desk until she was nearly sitting on it.

Tom's moans tasted *lovely* in my mouth. Her small hands were at my sides as I cupped her nape, swirling my tongue and finding my sanity there against her.

When my cock grew at her cute little noises, she broke the kiss to gasp, staring me down. Those eyes lingered on where my cock lay in wait, begging to escape my pants.

"Have you touched a man before, Tommelise?" I asked in a low tone, wanton with lust as she bit her goddamn lip again.

Normally, that sort of thing didn't do things to me; however, when *she* did it–game over. I tugged on her lip with my teeth, the sight driving me crazy, before groaning and pulling away from her reluctantly.

She shook her head in response to my question, and I closed my eyes to hold back.

"Has anyone *ever* touched *you?*" *I dared to ask.*

She bit her lip and shook her head.

Fuck.

"Tonight is your lucky night then, Tom," I promised, envisioning her with those legs wrapped tight around my fucking skull, squeezing me. I needed to hear more of those moans of hers.

She looked away coyly before meeting my stare.

Pulling her into me, I captured those sweet lips, tasting *home* amongst the trees. My tongue swirled with hers as my hands dropped to cup her ass, squeezing slightly. Her answering groan made me pull away, trailing kisses down her jaw and ending at her neck.

As I held her to me, cupping the back of her head, I began sucking on her neck, a soft sigh leaving her.

"Tell me what you want," I murmured, a quiet command before I consumed her.

"Please, Nel."

I growled low at the sound of my shortened name on her lips before burying my head into her neck, licking hard, her sweat tasting fantastic on my tongue. Her heart pulsated through her veins, reverberating in my eardrum. I felt her hand thrust into my hair before I kissed her soft skin.

"Say the words, sweetheart."

I leaned back to smirk, waiting.

"Touch me," her eyes fluttered open, looking hazy, "God, *please,* just touch me."

The plea fell from her lips as I pressed my straining cock against her. She released a hushed sound as I kissed her briskly, pulling away.

"Take off your dress and let me see you, little one," I whispered with seductive intent, resisting the urge to rip it off.

Pulling away slowly, she moved her straps off her shoulders and turned around, looking to the side as she pulled her hair over one shoulder.

"Will you unzip me?" Her tone was low when she spoke, and I was on it immediately, wasting no time.

I blew gently across her back and neck as I unzipped her, realizing she was bare underneath.

God, kill me now.

"You are a dangerous woman, after all," I whispered against her shoulder as her dress fell to the floor, pooling around her feet.

I trailed kisses down her spine until I reached her tiny, little ass and nibbled on her cheeks.

"Oh, my."

Hiding my smirk, I licked her cheek and forced her to turn around.

On my knees, I peered up at her once she faced me. I knew how those dogs felt before, kneeling before me and begging for my cock as I looked down upon them. There I was. *Funny how the tables have turned, but Tommelise was no dog.*

"Hop up onto the desk," I instructed as she did, inching her sweet ass onto my desk.

My god, would I be picturing this sight on repeat later.

I raised my brow when she kept her legs closed. "Open for me, let me taste you."

She tugged on her bottom lip, gaining more confidence as she spoke. "I've touched myself before, you know."

Amusement danced on my lips. "I knew you weren't completely innocent."

She smiled at me, slowly opening her legs and exposing her pink, little pussy. She swelled under my stare, her pussy weeping and ready for me. Famished for a taste, I moved closer, kissing her inner thighs.

"Show me how you touch yourself," I tell her softly, my tone dripping with need.

What are you doing to me, woman?

I watched in fascination as her two fingers worked her clit without much coaxing. She was already dripping wet. Amazed at the sight of the woman before me, I told her to put her hand in my hair and let me take care of the rest. I couldn't resist any longer as she panted and moaned from the pleasure she brought.

I placed her legs over my shoulders, licking up her cunt before teasing her hole and making my way to her clit in short strides.

My Little One tried to muffle her moan, but her hand in my hair gave her away as she tugged and pulled.

My eyes wandered upward to find her losing herself. Her head was tilted back, mouth agape with delicious sounds escaping. Her hand massaged her breast as the other gripped my desk.

How dare I neglect those.

I was so eager that I forgot all about teasing her first.

Later, perhaps, but I was a starving man blinded by the desire to please the woman on my tongue. And she tasted *so fucking good.* I was driven by an innate need to mate her right then and fuck her over my desk.

My hand reached up to cup and squeezed the breast she held with her flushed skin and pretty pink nipples. She was heaven incarnate if I believed in one before her—she was what I envisioned, with her naturally red hair and eyes so blue like the sea, I drowned in them. I'd drown in both her pussy and those eyes.

Lost in the pure taste of her, I felt her legs tighten until she began to shake on my tongue with a moan of my dreams.

I gave her that. *Me and me alone.*

Before I could give her another orgasm, she tried to push me away, shaking under my tongue's light touch.

"Your body is capable of more than one of those, you know…"

She sighed and leaned back, squirming and trying to get away as I held her firm.

"B-but—" I put my finger to her lips, consumed by how different and pure she tasted.

"One more, Little One," I encouraged, amused by the fact *she thought I was finished.* The bond buzzed underneath the surface of my skin, the insatiable need to pleasure and please my mate.

My hand moved back to her breast as she leaned further back on my desk, lying flat. Enjoying the view, I began to finger fuck her while imagining my cock filling her instead.

Gazing up at her, I placed her nipple in my mouth, twirling my tongue around her risen peak. Her hand clutched my hair as she bucked up with a strangled cry. I could feel her swell once more, strangling my fingers like she would soon be gripping my cock.

I moved my mouth immediately back to her clit, sucking out her soul. Her second orgasm found her faster than the first as I curled my fingers up into that perfect spot. Her scream of pleasure made me harder than ever before.

Tom would be my sanctuary and haven. My mate, to worship and taste.

One taste and I was already obsessed.

What the fuck is wrong with me?

I guess she had no clue she was my mate—*fated to a devil like me.*

Drinking down her juices and being reminded of what I was missing in life before meeting her, I looked up to find her spent and panting, trying to catch her breath. The scene of it had me spiraling further. I stood up and pressed my cock against where I wanted to be, and her head popped up from the desk.

"Touching yourself has nothing on my tongue, does it?" I asked, a smirk playing confidently on my lips.

She huffed a laugh, looking at where I ached the most. Her look turned hungry as she answered me, *"You are much better than my hand."*

Grinning with devious intent, Tom sat up fully. I wanted her to taste herself, so I snuck my tongue inside her mouth while teasing her breast with one hand and wrapping my other arm around her back.

"Now you get to taste how amazing you are," I told her while pulling away.

Her face flushed, and she scooted more off the desk.

"Will you show me how to pleasure you?" Her request was earnest, and my cock begged for this lesson.

"If you insist," I told her sweetly, my brain emptying all thoughts other than her lips wrapped around me.

Fucking hell.

Tom was down on her knees before I could even ask, unzipping my pants and pulling me out.

Her eagerness was my undoing, feeling my blood awaken and come to life, a faint magic in her touch.

"I'm generally…*rougher,* but I won't do that to you tonight, little one. My cock has a mind of his own when it comes to you, apparently."

Along with my mind.

A quick smile formed on her lips before she took me out completely, gasping at the sight. A gesture that made me feel unspeakable things as she took part of me into her mouth.

Her teeth lightly grazed me as she sucked, and I groaned at the sensation of her hot, wet mouth. I hadn't had my dicked sucked in a while either, so the old boy was ready for it.

Tom seemed eager, not that sucking cock was *hard.* However, my mate sucked my soul into her mouth. The sensation of her tongue and suction had my mind empty. All I could see was her painted pink lips wrapped around me and the soft humming sound coming from her. *Fuck me.*

I closed my eyes, enjoying the feeling, until she stopped to ask, "Is this okay?" She sounded so innocent and pure, it made me stiffer, my cock thickening at her words.

"Yes, don't stop, little one. Keep sucking with that sinful tongue," I told her before catching that sweet smile of hers, eliciting a grunt from me.

She wrapped her lips around my cock, flattening her tongue against the base, sucking. A groan fell from my lips as she wrapped her hands around my base fucking me with her mouth.

My soul was hers.

I wrapped my fingers in her hair as *I* began fucking her mouth. My cock hit the back of her throat, gagging her. Tom looked at me as tears spilled down her face, her pupils blown with desire.

"Breathe through your nose, little one, and relax your jaw." Tom hums on my cock as her mouth relaxes, allowing me to move faster. I felt the rush heading toward me faster than I would have liked. She looked so fucking good with her eyes closed, crying *for me.*

"That perfect mouth of yours, tasting me, too big to fill such a tiny space, but begging for more... So, fucking perfect," I praised, feeling my orgasm rise within while warning her in advance.

"Keep your jaw relaxed and open wide," I told her breathlessly while she did as instructed.

I tangled my fingers in her hair, fucking her mouth faster until I jolted as my cum spilled down her throat, and she took every last drop *like the good Little One she was.*

"God, look at you, so perfect and whole as I filled that sweet mouth. *So. Fucking. Perfect. Little. One.*"

A final moan flew out of me as I eased up, fondly running my hand through her hair.

Panting and catching my breath, I wiped those tears from her eyes and pulled her to her feet.

"You did amazing. I'm impressed, sweetheart." It was my turn to bite my lip, and I saw her focus on it before her smile melted me completely.

I took off my shirt before I scooped her up and sat with her in my oversized office chair.

"You told me about your life outside the city and your mother; now tell me all your favorite things. Your hopes. Your dreams…"

I listened as she told me about singing and dancing, her top two favorite things. She mentioned having a great birthday so far in the city and how being outdoors made her feel at peace…then she asked about *me.*

Strangely enough, I told her. It was comfortable there with her in my lap, running her fingers along my bare skin and mine stroking hers.

She belonged with me. *My mate.* I wondered if she knew what she was to me.

Tom touched my ear, seeing the small scar before kissing it gently.

The gesture broke me in a new way. No one had ever done that before. It made me feel vulnerable and exposed. Yet, Tom seemed happy to sit and chat with me while being naked in my lap. There were no worries of gold-digging whores or enemies trying to kill me then. It was just us in our own little world.

"I'm sorry. I must seem dull and privileged to you…"

I cupped her face, moving it gently for her to look at me. "Don't put words in my mouth. You are unlike *anyone* I've met." My heart thumped inside my ribcage as I took in those precious blue gems, "You're refreshing, sweetheart. Don't sell yourself short. You are worth more than my empire."

She blinked before moving closer to kiss the corner of my mouth.

"Then don't sell yourself short either," she told me as her eyes roved over my exposed torso. "You fought for your place and survived. That's an admirable quality, too."

I couldn't help my low chuckle. "I've never heard anyone tell that to a killer before."

She puffed her cheeks, pouting as I laughed until my belly ached. Her innocence was amusing. I showed her a different side of me that no one knew. Of course, she'd be naïve to my depravity and crimes. Tom was a farm girl, and my reality probably seemed foreign to her, something she could explain away by circumstance.

"I have something for you," I told her while reaching for my desk drawer to grab my mother's necklace, a promise to return no matter what may lie ahead.

I would never leave my mate behind if I could help it. I needed her to know that, too. The necklace symbolized what I lost and gained with my parents' deaths with a promise of a brighter future.

"I don't need anything—" I put my finger to her lips to silence her before fastening it around her neck. She looked fucking sinful wearing it nude while in my lap.

"It's a promise that I will return to you, and we'll see each other again after tonight. If you'll have me."

I gazed up into those curious, gorgeous blue eyes as she frowned, contemplating yet appreciating the gesture by how she fiddled with it in her tiny hands. I clasped mine over hers to get her to look at me.

"I don't know what to say…"

I kissed her nose playfully to remove her frown and doubts. Thankfully, it worked, and she began to giggle as I placed several scattered kisses across her cheeks and jaw, down to her neck.

She finally thanked me and returned the affection.

We continued that way for hours, losing track of time. Fate had led me straight *to her.* That's what the buzzing in the air was. The particles of time and space were bringing us together.

Something about Tom was filling my chest with a lightness unlike anything before. *The cage my heart was locked in.* One night was all it took for me. I would soon claim her completely.

She was mine.

Chapter 3

"I'm Not Going to Marry Your Son"

Chapter Playlist:
"Crystaleyes" by AViVA
"Dissolve" by Absofacto, NITESHIFT
"Night Vision" by Transviolet

Tom

It was an incredible birthday. All I could think about was Nelly's lips claiming my body and how those green eyes stayed on me the entire night. His hands were rough but tender, and the way he held me was a thing of dreams; his tongue was *sinful.* The rush of being with him brought me to new heights, and I knew I needed more.

Was I insane to entertain the idea of continuing to *hang out* with the crime king of the city? *Probably.*

Did I care? *Not one bit.*

Not with the way he spoke to me as if I was meant to be his, and I fell right into him. *As if I'd always belonged to him.*

I *could* stop, but after the best night of my entire life, why should I? Something unexplainable screamed within my blood that he held all the answers I sought. It roared within me; *he was mine.* In a consuming way, that said, *"Touch me, please me—love me."*

And the simple but gorgeous necklace? *So sweet!* I toyed with the gold chain on my neck, gazing at the green gem that reminded me of his eyes. It was a gift from Nelly—a promise to return to me.

I moved around my room and tucked it fondly between my fingers as I thought of him, smirking from ear to ear as I dreamed of his eventual return to my house. It had been a couple of days already, and he hadn't left my mind since. I dreamed of more. *To be fucked,* as he said, and those filthy words gave rise to the heat within me and the blush to my cheeks.

I told my mother all about him, minus the criminal and killing parts. *Doubt she would approve.* I mentioned how he'd stop by later that week, and my mother *seemed* happy about it. She did tell me to be careful, as men loved to take advantage of women, but I should follow where my heart led me.

Nothing was impossible, Tom.

A few more days and nights passed, and I still floated on a dreamy, naïve cloud where Nelly consumed my thoughts. His dark red hair and deep, sultry voice made me slick between my thighs as I awaited his return. Until then, I'd enjoy the memories swirling of the first night I had with him. *All the dirty, filthy things that he had awakened in me.*

To keep myself busy, I helped my mother like usual, tending to the animals on the farm, feeding the chickens, and brushing the horses. My mother's smile would catch me off guard, at times. She would say how much *brighter* my smile was and how precious the gift of new love was.

When I went to bed one night, I heard my dog snoring nearby on his bed. I called him Oreh.

He was a lazy but suitable dog, and I loved him with all I had. All he wanted were his scratches and pets.

Closing my eyes to try and sleep, I did my best to quiet my mind and sleep despite the sounds Oreh made like he was a snoring bear in hibernation. Just when I had almost drifted off to sleep, I heard something scrape against the window.

Awareness made my eyes pop open. It was not a dream as I tucked myself more under the covers. My heartbeat rebounded loudly in my ears as fear overtook me.

The window slammed open, and two masked people jumped inside, looking around before seeing me in bed. Panic shot through me as I wrestled with silence or alerting my dog. The people looked at each other before charging towards me.

They grabbed me as I called for my dog, "Or-eh!"

Struggling against the masked people's grip, they hoisted me out of bed. Oreh jumped up and began barking, but it wasn't enough to alert my mother in time.

Cursing inwardly at myself as fear made me scream, a cloth bag was thrown over my head before I was tossed over someone's shoulder. I kicked and yelled to the best of my ability, hearing grunts and curses.

It was then I felt a sharp pain as something hit the back of my head, and it all went dark.

A pounding headache awoke me with a deep, rumbling groan. It was disorienting as I tried to open my eyes but quickly shut them when it hurt to keep them open. My head fell back as I realized I was sitting up…*tied to a chair.*

I forced my eyes open, the room spinning on its axis. Trying to remain calm, I focused on my surroundings despite the pain and dizziness.

A table was hidden in a dark corner, and a single bright light remained on me, doing nothing to spare the pain in my head.

My eyes adjusted to the table I could vaguely make out. Smoke came from a slender hand; long fingers with intense red polish held the stick. The figure moved slightly, watching from the dark.

"Good, you're awake," a woman's voice echoed out as I jumped, not expecting the person to speak. Her accent was one I couldn't place as I saw the flick of an ember from the shadow of a hand.

Waiting a long moment, I decided to ask the obvious question, *"Why am I here?"*

My voice sounded froggy, croaking out the question. My throat was dry, and I wondered how long I had been in that chair. It was dark and damp, and hard to pinpoint where the hell I was.

The embers went out as smoke eased out from the shadows as if preparing me for a monster coming out of the dark.

That's when the woman eased out of the shadows, unmasking the figure before me. She was slim in a shiny, short red dress with unblemished skin. Her makeup was overdone, and her hair was a vivid green, reminding me of some of the toads I had seen outside. *A toad in a pretty woman's skin.*

A sly smirk appeared on her face, making her look odd, and I wondered if she *was* a toad, a shifter of some sort. I held my breath for a tongue to pop out and grab a fly. *I might throw up.*

"I found what that fae king desires most, *so I took it from him.* He may think he reigns, but many of us bide our time in the shadows," she paused, her look becoming darker as if she were changing from the disguise of a pretty woman to a toad. Maybe it was a trick of the light or my vision trying to still adjust.

Fear flooded me as I shook, noticing how she moved closer. My hands cramped up from being tied behind me, aching from the pull of the binds. I was trapped with no way out.

"You have potential though, so now I will make use of you here instead of killing you," she continued, slithering closer like a snake, her fake disguise wearing thin as a feeling arose within me that something dreadful would happen, more terrifying than being taken in the night.

So, Nelly's enemies were now *my enemies, unfortunately for me.*

I leaned my head back and tried to focus on *anything* other than whatever the woman had planned for me, struggling against the ties that bound me.

The woman grabbed my face suddenly, making me look at her face, a sneer lingering there.

"I have been trying to get one over on Nelly, you see, and to my delight, *there you were, a prize to be taken and regifted. He'll never have you now. You belong to me.*"

This wasn't good, *not at all.* My eyes went wide as she laughed in my face.

"So, *pathetic,*" her grip tightened as I winced, her dark eyes staring into mine, "If you want to remain alive, you will strip at our club and marry my son, Led."

I tried to move my head from her grip, but the room began to spin again as I blinked my eyes open and closed to focus on her face, appearing more and more like a toad.

Her nails dug into my skin as she continued with her threats, "You will be trained, and if you try to escape, we will kill your mother. *No one will miss you. You belong to me—us now.* Nelly doesn't get to own this city and get the girl too," she nearly snarled in my face as I winced, "Fortunately for you, my son is decent looking but isn't the smartest... They're all idiots, and I run this show here. You will love and marry him, or I'll deliver your corpse to Nelly as a *gift* should you try me."

Struggling more, I broke free of her grip.

"I'm not going to marry your son," I protested though I was trembling with fear, and she *laughed.* Her hand found its way across my face, forcefully sending my head to the side. The force of it had the room rotating around me.

"Why did you think you had a choice, deary? You're my leverage for more power. If I happen to be wrong about you, then I will simply kill you. It is no loss either way, but I see a profit, as you are pretty enough. Maybe it's that exotic red hair you have. A fae trait."

I tried to blink away the blur of the room as my ears pounded a sense of looming dread resounding in my veins. I didn't have time to think over her words as a hazy vision of her slid away back into the shadows before coming back into the light, igniting a stick, and placing it into her mouth.

"It's a cigarette. Do you want one?" She offered, and I frowned, shaking my head, wracking my brain on how to stay alive.

All I knew was that I had to protect myself and survive. I would not be the cause of my mother's death. *I had to agree.*

The green-haired toad blew out smoke, "Tom is not a sexy name, so for the stage, I will give you a fake name. *Fay* seems suitable enough," she snickered as a bleary realization dawned on me. She was implying that I was like Nelly, *which I'd think about later.* "Cooperate and you'll live to see another day. Understood?"

It was a warning. With how menacing her features became, I couldn't help the hard swallow down my throat. This woman made me nervous about what would come next.

Narrowing her eyes, she took another puff of her cigarette and put it out on my neck abruptly.

I wrestled my binds, screaming in pain as she tossed it cruelly, laughing and slinking back into the shadows before I heard a door close.

Her laughter echoed eerily until it finally faded. My breathing was uneven as my thoughts raced, trying to register the situation and the burning sensation in my neck. *Fae, toads, enemies, and a new life that I didn't ask for.*

When the threats dawned on me, a sob left my lips, realizing that Nelly wouldn't find me, and no one knew where I was. The toad woman ran the show, and I had to comply; otherwise, I'd meet my maker along with my mother. Feeling defeated, my head hung over my legs, my future in chains.

Finally, I saw those bright dreams of the city for what they were, monsters in nightmares. I was naïve to think I could get a fairytale like the ones I read about with mates and supernatural creatures. There would be no consuming kisses or ravaging touches across my lovers' skin.

It was too little too late now. All that lay ahead was doom and I had to comply for survival with that toad woman under the guise of a pretty dress and makeup.

Would Nelly look for me after not finding me at home? Or was it a fool's errand, and I misread the connection I felt? I could still remember the electric current grazing me from head to toe the minute he touched me. I battled my mind about whether the king and his resources would find me, but sitting there alone under the singular light, I knew I had to rely on myself.

Glancing sideways away from the light above me, my tears dissipated.

There was no use in fighting my current fate. Whether Nelly found me or not, at that moment, I held no power.

I would submit to the dangerous woman if only to spare my mother. Memories of her kind smile would get me through whatever happened next. It was always her and I. I didn't trust the woman or her intentions, but I had a deep, unsettling feeling that she would keep her promises. Wondering how to begin to make light of the situation, the only positive I could find was staying alive long enough to escape my new prison someday.

Chapter 4

"I'm Coming For You, Sweetheart"

Chapter Playlist:
"Bootleg Blood" by Thief
"Fracture" by Apashe, Flux Pavilion, Joey Valence & Brae
"Jaded" by Betcha
"In One Ear" by Cage The Elephant

Nelly

Tommelise was *taken*.

I paced around my office and waited anxiously days beforehand. Buz was probably tired of me talking about Tom being my mate, yet his grin told me he wasn't.

"*I can't wait to meet her,*" he had said during one of *many conversations*.

I shoved his shoulder, hiding my smirk as I did everything to pass the time by checking on my properties and the tedious paperwork of the businesses.

When the time came, I went to her house as promised and found her mother crying on the stoop. Immediately, I knew something was wrong. Her hair covered her face, her face in her hands as I walked over slowly, purposely making noise with the crunching of my shoes on the rocky path to her. She looked up at me with red cheeks and swollen eyelids from crying. I introduced myself to her, and she choked out another sob, mumbling how Tommelise was taken.

Dread pooled in my belly as I asked her to explain, and I was there to help. I placed a comforting hand on her shoulder before she showed me around Tom's room. She looked as if she hadn't slept, and my heart struggled in my chest, the bond within roaring to protect and defend her daughter.

She lingered in the doorway to her room as I observed the disarray around me. The bed was messy, glass littered the floor, and random objects were strewn all around. A storm had blown through her room, and my gaze roved over until it settled on the medium-sized spotted mutt in the corner, whining softly as if the dog were crying over the situation, too.

"His name is Oreh, and his barking alerted me that something was wrong," I heard her whisper from behind me, sniffling. I sighed, moving over to pet him.

Masked toads, they took her.

The words echoed faintly in my mind, and I blinked, tilting my head. Was I insane, or did I just *hear* the dog's thoughts? Madness must have claimed me, after all.

Just fucking great.

To humor myself, I *asked* him, "Did people in masks take her away, Oreh?"

The mutt grunted a short bark and then whined.

Okay, so I can fucking talk to dogs now? Is this one of the fae gifts I ignored, or have I truly lost it?

Shaking myself out of my spiraling thoughts over *who* kidnapped my mate, I lightly patted his head and scratched behind his ears.

Oreh seemed to appreciate the gesture and comfort.

Thank you. Please find her.

I nodded to a *dog.*

Something itched under the surface of my skin, a familiar need to have blood rain over the city streets. It wasn't the only thing stirring as magic and the bond pulled at me. A string of fate and my heritage I ignored for so many years. It was awakening and thrumming back to life within me.

I was beginning to feel the start of a spiral—wherever it would drag me to. Anger shook my body as I looked towards the broken window, a breeze caressing through the room. I knew what needed to happen, instinct taking over me.

"I'll find her and bring her back, Oreh," I promised him while standing up, turning to catch Tom's mother watching me curiously.

Reiterating what I told the dog, I spoke back to her. Doubt pooled in those blue eyes that reminded me of my newest reason to exist. Tom's face flashed in my mind as I left her mom's farmhouse after promising her to return with an update soon. I practically teleported myself through the woods back to my car. My magic was coming back to life, whether I wanted it to happen or not.

Rage had me gripping the steering wheel, clenching my jaw over the realization of the toads becoming a problem for me *again. I should've fucking known they'd find a way into my domain.*

While her mother didn't *say* it was my fault she got taken, *there was a prickling sensation of accusation aimed at the back of my head.*

What Tom's mother didn't know was that I wasn't one to be trifled with, and I'd find her. Bodies would line the pathway to her. *One way or another.*

The doors slammed open when I stormed into my club, which was nearly vacant except for Buz and a few of the guys.

"Pull the cameras, now," I barked.

Buz set his glass of dark liquid down as my guys stood at attention.

"Cousin, what's wrong?" Buz asked with worry in his tone.

So, I told him, and the guys were all at attention, moving in various directions to roam the city and help search for my mate.

"We need to review the cameras from that night, days before and after," I told him as we rushed to the security room that was housed underneath the club.

"See who left and entered the building, any suspicious cars or people, then get the guys to look into it. It will take some time, but we should begin immediately." He agreed, using his fingerprint to open the door once we made it there.

Looking at me over his shoulder, I nodded my head in agreement, demanding I be a part of it.

"No problem, boss. I'll get it pulled up for you. How far from that night do you want to begin?" He asked, leaning over a keyboard with the plethora of screens lining the wall.

"I'll start with two weeks. Can't be too careful. The last new hires occurred then, so that seems like a good starting point," I told him, sitting in a comfortable chair to begin.

"Good thinking, Nel. While you check out the club's footage, I'll use my software and hack into the city's cameras," he spoke, getting us started with footage he pulled up for me. "I'll make some calls for our guys to look into the people we hired recently to see if we can get a thorough review too. They could have applied under aliases."

Fuck!

Rubbing my temples in frustration, I took a deep, steadying breath. "Good."

Staring at the glowing screens in front of me, he slid over the master keyboard, picked up his phone, and searched another computer not linked to the screens in front of me for the trail of new hires.

Stretching my back, I clicked a button and leaned back in the chair, settling in for the long days of footage ahead.

Over the following weeks, my eyes strained and ached over the endless, boring footage, but Buz and I remained glued to those screens. We eventually found cars we didn't recognize near the club and inside my domain. We officially confirmed the trail back to the toads. We traced one of the hidden identities of the new hires, the *toad momma*. The one who led that fucking family.

When I realized one of the bartenders was her in disguise with another name, I threw the keyboard at the opposite wall, away from the screens.

"Fuck!" I shoved the chair away, my hands gripping my hair tight as Buz stood.

Those fucking toads sticking their grimy hands where they didn't belong. They were the bane of my existence. It has always been a power struggle with them since the beginning. They thought they could sneak into *my* territory and claim *my girl?*

Over my dead body. There would be hell to pay. They wouldn't see me fucking coming.

And if a hair on her head was harmed? *Game the fuck over.*

Buz's hand landed on my shoulder, trying to ground me back to the planet, and my eyes flared toward him.

"We know *who* has her. Now it's just a matter of *where.* We'll get her, boss, but we need to do it right. Give me some time to infiltrate their operation and find where they have her. *We will find her.*"

I exhaled, willing myself to trust him with the safety of my mate. "I don't want any of us to get killed in the process. We can't go guns-blazing in their territory without starting a war. Give me two weeks."

"*Two* weeks? Are you fucking kidding me?" I screeched, pulling away from him to throw something else, "Too much time has passed already!"

"Have I ever let you down before?" His eyes never left mine when I did a complete 180 to face him again.

I struggled to contain myself, my magic edging closer to the surface as we stared each other down. He broke away from our staring contest first while I anxiously rubbed my throbbing temples.

"No," I said with defeat.

"Alright then, let's do this right. We'll do it my way to reduce casualties and ensure she returns safely. If things go south with them, then you can rain blood. I recommend doing something to keep your magic from wreaking havoc unintentionally. Channel it, remind it that it doesn't own you. It's been locked away for too long, Nelly."

I offered the hint of a smile as he shook his head, holding back a laugh.

"You're right. You always know the *magic* words to get my mind back on track, let's fucking get them."

Buz answered me with a grin of his own, patting my shoulder as we left his tech room to get to work. Over the years, Buz figured out when to back off and when to center me when my rage boiled over, especially when I begged to bathe in my enemies' blood.

He knew if I didn't participate somehow, I'd go out of my fucking mind and impulsively take things into my own hands.

Keep her safe. It was the only thought that roared in my mind, and Buz had to keep reminding me when I got fidgety and anxious.

To keep me grounded even more, I ended up going through meditation practices, trying to quiet my mind. Figuring out how to channel my magic was even more unnerving. It was like opening the attic of an old house and finding all sorts of things buried under the dust.

I spent a lot of time in nature, lighting campfires with my fingertips and making plants grow. Sometimes, the trees would turn greener, or what was once dead would be full of life again. It felt like I was finding myself again, and in between figuring out my magic, I returned to Tom's house frequently. I needed to ensure her mother was still safe and assisted with the animals and heavy lifting. *They talked to me in their minds about mindless things, thanking me for helping Tom's mother and them.*

Listening to animals speak to me was mind-numbing, but eventually, I learned to quiet my mind. Tom's mother even warmed up to me, and the look of doubt was eventually washed from her face. She began to sleep more and trusted me that I would find Tom. I left out the dirty details, of course, but I made myself useful, helping her clean up the chaos that lay in Tom's room from when she was taken. Her scent still lingered in the air; I found it motivating and the bond led me to do all I could to find her.

My men and I paid particular attention to *who* came into my domain. Security was upped, and I had my people do thorough searches and extra background checks for the workers in *The Parisian* and my other spots in town. There couldn't be any more fucking mistakes and errors.

I was paranoid and overdoing it, but it was my fault for *letting* it happen. I was supposed to protect and seal our bonds. *I* did this to myself and her.

How could I be so careless as to lose myself so much with her, knowing that I had the enemies I did? Enemies who would exploit any weakness.

Stupid, fucking idiot.

I'd hate myself forever if anything happened to her, but I'd seek redemption in blood if I had to. Then, I would beg at her feet for the rest of my life for forgiveness.

My mate was alone out there, fending for herself, which scared me more than anything. My biggest fear was how my enemies would break and mold her sweetness and take away her innocence. They fed off that shit. I may be twisted, but I didn't fuck with trafficking as they did. *Or kidnapping innocents.* There was *some* sanity in all my madness.

My anger, when it went unchecked, caused me to be impulsive. It had gotten to that point as more weeks went by with no progress made, and something inside me snapped.

Had we forged our mate bond completely with sex, I would have her. With the mate connection, we would always find our way back to each other through telepathy and the pull of such powerful bonds. I had already felt hints of it during our first night together, pulling me harder and deeper into such a fateful connection.

I plotted how I'd rain blood in their territory once we found her specific location. I'd really lose it if they hurt her in any way. I somehow already knew the answer, so I mentally planned their deaths and all the torturous ways to make them suffer as Tom probably did.

Hold on, Tommelise, I'm coming for you, sweetheart.

Chapter 5

"Am I Safe?"

Chapter Playlist:
"GDFR (feat. Sage the Gemini & Lookas)" by Flo Rida, Sage The Gemini, Lookas
"In The Night" by The Weeknd
"High" by Zella Day
"Conscious" by BROODS
"Deep End" by Ruelle

Tom

The lights were low, and sultry music began before the beat increased. The pole was shining like a beacon to the audience as I rolled my hips, stalking towards it. I ignored the faces in the crowd while I seeped into the space of dancing as my hands wrapped around the pole, and I began to climb it like a conquest.

My skin was bare, minus the tassels covering my nipples and my red thong. Shouts and hollers echoed through the room as I spun around in tune with the music, gyrating my hips toward the pole as if it were a cock.

Upside down, the dollar bills flew and rained down my bare body as I moaned for the supernaturals who could hear me. When the song and routine ended, I gathered the money sending sweet, flirtatious smiles out to the crowd, and more was tucked in my thong before my ass was smacked.

As if summoned by the sound, *Led* gathered the money with his grimy hands, eager to collect it from me.

"You did well. You go on again in an hour as the most exotic redhead. Continue giving them a show, and then tonight, *it's my turn with you.*"

Offering a fake smile, I nodded as he disappeared.

Creep.

My body was a vessel to be used as they saw fit.

Stripping was easier than I thought, and the more I did it, the more the green-haired bitch left me alone. Her son, on the other hand, *not so much.*

The Toads took my necklace and my hope with it. None of her sons were charming and Led threatened them if they touched me. While he reserved me for himself, he *loved* sharing me with his friends.

I was disgusted with myself early on, but then it sank in fully that I needed to survive and protect my mother. So, I learned to be useful, becoming a husk of a woman. A body without a mind.

My only escape was dancing to the music and basking in the praise from the crowd. It didn't mean anything to me when it came from the toad family, but it did when it came from strangers.

"Fuck, you're so hot."

"I love redheads."

"What a pretty mouth you have…"

"That's it, give us a show, gorgeous girl."

"I wish that pole was my dick."

My smile would grow from such words. As weird as it sounded, it gave me the fuel I needed when I wanted to give up.

Nelly's smile and green eyes still haunted me in my dreams, but eventually, I stopped seeing him there once the drugs pulled me into darkness. Led began dosing me weeks after my training began, pulling me into an induced bliss to deal with the abusive prison around me.

None of them cared about what happened to me. *I brought them money*

"Come see, the exotic Fay," flashed in neon letters—*advertising me as if I were a show-horse.* I rolled my eyes inwardly. *Whatever, at least I lived another day.*

Perhaps that's all I was to them, other than a mockery toward Nelly. *At least I was good enough for something.*

Eventually, they stopped hiding that they had me. They *wanted* Nelly to see that they had his prize.

Hazy euphoria swept my vision, numbing me to the world around me and enabling me to survive better. Memories swirled in the back of my mind somewhere in between me being aware and frolicking in my haze.

I vaguely recalled one evening when Led was too drunk to get it up, and *Momma Toad, as I called her,* walked in, drunk, too.

Her speech was slurred as she mentioned something, and all I picked up on was, "You're of fae descent."

I pretended I didn't hear her as I was tangled between limbs on the bed. She was intoxicated and probably spouting lies just to get a reaction out of me.

"I met several others before..." I heard her stumble around, trying to move closer to me as snores floated from the bed, "Fae look like you and that king."

Whatever the hell that means.

Where the hell were the other faeries? Was my father one? *Were the fae cruel and not whimsical and magical as I once hoped and read about?*

It wouldn't be the first dream of mine to die that I would experience. *Or the last.*

As disappointing as it was to think about, *the toads* made me believe I was only good for *one night.* Why would I believe in anything different?

Numbness was all I allowed myself to feel, and I needed it to carry me through.

Days and nights meshed together; nothing mattered to me. I worked the pole, danced, received my desired praises from the crowd, and serviced Led with whoever else.

On one particular night, once the drugs seeped into my bloodstream, I vaguely remembered Led rolling away from me to dress.

His voice was distorted as he spoke, *"I have to go out, be good while I am gone."*

Patting my head, I pretended to be asleep while he dressed and left the room. I was unsure how much time I waited before I rolled onto the floor, nearly hitting my head on the nightstand. Groaning at the impact, I crawled on the floor as the room spun.

Focus, Tom, focus!

Maybe it was sheer will, but I managed to pull myself up, using a chair to sustain my weight. My vision became less blurry, even if the room was spinning. Stumbling to the door, not caring what night slip I had on or how much was shown, I made my way out of the room. It was complicated to remember where I was or how to leave Led's area when all the doors and hallways looked the same, a maze to my incoherent mind.

I trudged through, hanging onto the walls and openings as I made my way into the maze of dim lights and lingering shadows.

Nervousness kept me frantically moving, for I feared getting caught and killed in the act of trying to escape.

Somehow, a stroke of fate, I supposed, I opened a door and fell out into the street.

Air, fresh air.

I choked out a silent cry of relief, fueling me forward to stand up, leaning against the brick of a building. Slowly and clumsily, I ran down the path toward the light at the end, hoping I'd find my way out.

The sunset swirled in my vision as I tried to make out the darkening streets with their neon signs, morphing and shaping themselves into odd shapes.

Please, let me make it out.

Stumbling around the streets, a few people called my stage name and tried to corner me. I somehow escaped them by the skin of my teeth, making my way away from the blinding lights.

I couldn't see in my unstable state and tripped, falling into some sort of waterway. I didn't know how to fucking swim.

Crying out, a current pulled me under and away from wherever I was. I held my breath, hoping that my death would be swift and less painful than however long I was with my captors.

While trying to breathe and keep my head above water, images of dark red hair flooded my mind and my lungs. A smirking face and perfect green eyes flashed. A connection filling my veins, craving to be completed. Did Nelly forget about me? Was his interest in me a mere dream? Did he think of me as some whore, too?

After the time apart, I wouldn't blame him. I was no longer innocent or pure.

Torn out of my random thoughts, the current swept me to the surface briefly to take another breath and scream for help before being pulled back under as I flailed my arms about.

There was endless weightlessness as darkness filled my vision, bubbles leaving my lips. Which way was up or down?

When I thought it was over while my lungs were burning from lack of air, a hand grabbed mine, trying to pull me out.

The current was much too strong. Whoever it was ended up falling in with me until we were both pulled deeper. Their hand never left mine as I inhaled water and lost consciousness.

"She's alive," someone exclaimed. A male voice, *I think*.

My lungs were on fire, and my head was fuzzy. There was a sense of weightlessness right before I felt the hard ground underneath me.

When I came to fully, I choked and coughed up water while vaguely making out shadows standing around me before my eyes squeezed shut.

"Thank fucking god," someone else voiced, feeling someone *else* rubbing my back.

"That's it, Love, get the water out of you," the person at my back spoke.

"I didn't realize she couldn't swim... *I fucked up, guys,*" another male spoke, sounding distraught, "We almost lost our mate."

My head was reeling from the water and rushing air to my lungs. I was still dizzy despite my eyes being closed, struggling to remember how to breathe properly once the water emptied from me.

Wait, did they say, *mate? Our* mate?

What the hell?

Before I knew it, my eyes were opening again, and all I saw was a cloudy sky above me. Lost in some sort of dreamlike state, I realized I could breathe and see clearly—*no drugs;* I was somehow alive. What a relief.

Then, I recalled the male voices from before and wondered if I made it up all in my head.

It was probably the drugs, Tom. Of course, that's all it was.

I jumped when a voice lured me out of my foggy mind state.

"Are you okay, Tommelise?" A brown-haired male at my right asked, coming more into my field of vision.

I stared at the stranger above me, noticing two other identical males, minus their eyes I couldn't quite make out at the distance.

"How do you know my name?" I croaked out, wondering where my voice went and why I sounded like a damn toad.

The three of them hesitantly looked at one another, saying nothing at first.

Uhh, okay?

"*We* are witches, or warlocks, whatever you prefer," the one in the middle answered as the one at his right continued, "This city likes to use them interchangeably. Not the smartest bunch, no offense."

I said nothing as I closed my eyes, feeling overwhelmed. Ignoring the words spoken, not entirely caring *what* they were, the only important question I needed to know left my lips.

"Are we... *Am I safe?*"

"For now," another male at my left answered while I peeked over at him, not realizing he was beside me.

Why the hell were there so many men around me?

Feeling uncomfortable at the thought, awareness spread through me. What did these men want?

I hesitantly took the four men in, seeing their faces change to that of concern. *I don't think they mean harm.*

Trying to keep that in the back of my mind, I focused on taking in the male on my left. He was crouched next to me, wearing simple clothes like that of people I'd seen in the city. Raven hair sat disheveled on his head yet soft-looking with mesmerizing brown and orange eyes. I wondered why his eyes looked as they did… Was he a supernatural creature of some sort, too?

The longer I looked at him, the more I saw his face soften like he was already familiar with me. Lost in our staring contest, the man tucked my hair away from my face. The gesture was kind enough, but a flashback from the past weeks made me flinch once my brain caught up.

As if noticing my reaction, the guy frowned, "We won't hurt you." His frown deepened into a more troubled look as he contemplated what to say next, "I'm sorry. I'm sure you went through a lot, but you're safe now." His brown and orange eyes flickered, changing to a more intense orange briefly before resuming to brown.

How oddly charming.

I released a breath I didn't realize I was holding.

Letting his words wash over me, I muttered, "I wasn't sure what your intent was," I sighed, closing my eyes to block out the blurred flashes of my escaped prison, "and I need time…"

The guy gave me an empathetic look with a slight nod. Remembering their earlier words, *at least I think I remembered,* I blurted out, "Did I hear all of you properly? *Did you say something about being mates earlier, or was that a dream?"*

The gentleman offered a hand to help me sit up. I stared at it, deciding to accept before I jolted at the electricity at his touch. We had a moment of recognition as my eyes widened.

What the hell!

He nodded in confirmation, "I wasn't sure until I grabbed your hand…" The guys looked between themselves as if they were solving a problem.

"So?" I asked again, my heart picking up its pace. With the way my skin felt at his contact, an intuitive feeling told me I already knew the answer.

Locking eyes with the guy who still didn't let go of my hand, he exhaled slowly.

"Yes."

I stared into his gorgeous eyes, appreciating his honesty, yet a headache began to settle between my eyes. I'd figure out the mate thing later, and process it...

"O-ok. Well, introduce yourselves then, so it's not *weird.*"

What else was I supposed to say to that? I just found out I had mates–plural. The thought made me warm up again with a hope I had long forgotten. I had a feeling Nelly's connection wasn't a coincidence.

"I am Jac, a bird shifter," the guy beside me spoke, offering me a boyish smile as I registered a name with his handsome face. "I generally choose a crow or raven as I scour the skies, in case you're wondering... Anyway," he gestured the triplet-looking guys to my right, releasing my hand. My gaze followed as he introduced them.

The men kneeled next to me, and Quinn, Flynn, and Lynn were in order from left to right.

Since they were closer to me, I could take them in more. They were built the same, shapely, easy on the eyes, with dark hair that wasn't as messy as Jac's. The men began to grin at me as I took them in fully. Quinn had vibrant blue eyes, a different hue than my own yet nonetheless captivating. I could see his helpfulness and care in his gaze. Next to him, a pair of violet eyes stared into mine. They were so fascinating for such an odd color; I had never seen before. Before I could get lost in them, I found myself looking at Lynn, who had a unique mixture of gray that I found to be as breathtaking as the sky above me. Cloudy gray skies, that's what I saw when I looked at him.

"Well, then..." I moved my eyes away from the triplets, adjusting myself as I looked off into the distance before me, hearing the water ebb in its flow, "I suppose it's nice to meet you?"

So, these men weren't a danger *and were stunning,* but *mates?*

I stared at them in trepidation, not fully trusting them quite yet. "Tell me more about you." I indicated my head toward the witches without looking at them.

"Well, we're wanderers, I suppose, and we are free-spirited. We *know* things, and we disappear. Any place we travel, we make our home," Lynn spoke so softly that I turned to look at him.

We locked eyes as a sense of trust permeated the air between us. Part of me wondered if it was magic or *being mated* to make such a feeling occur, but before I could ponder further, his hand stretched toward me, offering to help me up.

The guys moved back and away as I took his hand without question, appreciating those hues of gray up close. Familiar tingles traveled up my arm, spreading throughout my body. *This must be a mate thing.* I felt the same with Nelly when we touched each other. *I guess they were my mates.*

I thanked him as the others hovered, making sure I was okay and steady *after nearly dying. Or did I die?*

"Are you three triplets..."

The three men sighed, looking between one another as Flynn stepped closer, answering the question. Violet eyes latched onto me as my brain scrambled to figure out just how in the hell would I be able to keep up with all of them. The unique eye colors would take some getting used to, but it wasn't necessarily a bad thing either.

"Well, our soul is split into three," he gestured between his two other counterparts, "we're the same, but we're not. It's a...*witch thing.* If you ever meet our mother, she'll be happy to explain, but we'd rather avoid that since she's a wicked woman who would probably split *your* soul into three without asking permission... I don't recommend it."

The guys winced as if remembering their mother all too well. I shrugged, not understanding, but I turned to look at Jac.

"Thank you for trying to save me..."

He offered me a smile, seeming uncomfortable. The air around us changed, no longer feeling at ease. Before I could ask why the sudden mood had changed, Jac began to talk.

"We shouldn't linger too much longer here. It's safe right now, but I'm unsure how much longer. We should leave.

What's close by?" He looked at the other three men as they nodded their heads in unison behind them.

Feeling weird vibes about the topic change, the triplets began to lead us away, and I certainly wasn't about to argue over safety.

"We're staying in neutral territory," one said from behind me.

"A circus, of all places," one of them said from beside me. I looked, seeing Quinn as he offered a friendly smile.

Wondering just what my life had become, I giggled.

Quirky witches, a circus, a bird shifter, multiple mates, wherever Nelly was—anything else?

Realizing I probably looked crazy, sinking into a fit of giggles, one of them began to ask, "Are you okay?"

"I'm sorry." *I wasn't because it was all too ridiculous.* "I'm laughing because I was held captive after meeting a fae *king*, suffering in said captivity and barely escaping. *Then,* I nearly drowned and found out I had multiple mates... It all sounds *crazy.*"

"You did drown, Love," Flynn frowned as we all stopped walking to stare at each other. Whatever I was about to say disappeared from my mind. I stood there frozen, unable to comprehend his words. *Died? Truly?*

"We brought you back to life with our magic," Lynn mentioned so quietly, the lighter gray in his eyes darkened as if a storm cloud was rolling in.

That's new.

Distracted by the sight of it, my gaze flicked over to where Flynn stood while staring off into the distance, "Teleporting would be an option, but we used *a lot* of power, so unfortunately, we have to make our way through part of the city again on foot."

I closed my eyes, sighing heavily at the realization of my ridiculous life but also feeling grateful I had other mates. Still, the pull of Nelly beckoned me even from the distance, and the desire to complete all the mate bonds overwhelmed me. I couldn't have one without the other and live soundly.

"Is Nelly okay?" It was all I could think to ask after thanking the triplets for saving me. *Or was being resurrected the better word for it?*

Violet eyes landed on me. "He's storming the strip club right now," Flynn said with a sigh, "and there's going to be a war in the streets. We'll have to be careful. We will go to him after we regain our strength and the violence subsides."

He stared off into the distance again, frozen as if he were watching it play out live.

"Shouldn't we go to his aid?" I asked, feeling oblivious.

Flynn shook his head, "We're much too weak and would be no use. We have enough energy to walk but not enough to defend our mate or protect him. Magic regeneration takes time. It takes even longer when we bring back the dead. *I'm sorry if that disappoints you, Love.*"

I took a steady breath, taking in his words. As much as we wanted to help him, we were in no position to. Yet, I couldn't help my worry as I rubbed my forehead. Even though the circumstances were related to him and I being seen together at *The Parisian*, I *didn't* blame him for any of it. Maybe that made me the biggest fool.

But he came back for me. My heart was torn by that fact alone.

"It's not your fault," I whispered, my heart aching over my next words, "I just want to be useful, and I don't feel like I am."

Quinn was at my side, rubbing my upper arm in comfort. "Being alive is more than useful; you don't need to do anything other than that."

"I don't ever want to experience that pain again," Lynn voiced quietly from the other side of me.

My brows furrowed as I frowned, the energy in the air shifting again, unsettling me. We needed to press onward.

"Well, let us go then. I'm wary of staying," I spoke, trying to redirect the mood and movement of all of us.

Jac gently touched my shoulder, rubbing his thumb in comfort. "I'm going to fly ahead and scout for any potential problems. I'll try and catch up with you all later. I can't wait to see you again, mated lover." He said the last part in a low purring tone that caused goosebumps to erupt across my skin and down my spine. *That was a promise, too.*

I offered him a sincere smile, taking it upon myself to kiss his cheek in thanks while wishing him safe travels.

He winked before disappearing, and when I blinked, I noticed a large black bird flying over us. It was such an incredulous sight; I couldn't tear my eyes away from it.

"That never gets old," Quinn smirked as the guys agreed, leading me away from the riverbank once Jac disappeared beyond the trees.

To pass the time as we walked, they asked me to talk about growing up, which was no doubt a distraction from the intense day.

We walked and talked for hours, getting to know one another. I explained my upbringing with my mother, and they explained how their mother was a greedy queen in their realm. She wanted more children for heirs, which was why she split their soul into three to create more powerful heritage lines. I still couldn't wrap my mind around it, and I hoped I wouldn't ever have to meet her *or find out for myself.*

My inner turmoil and hesitancy decreased the more we settled into our conversation. The triplets were not out to harm me, and it was a relief. Tension slowly eased out of me, a welcome sensation since being kidnapped for however long I had been gone.

My steps became heavier the more I realized I died, and the witches' powers were depleted. They must be exhausted, too. I hoped that once they were at full strength again, I could ask them for directions to my mother's house, assuming she was still alive. I'd never forgive myself if something happened to her.

Once they realized I had slowed down completely, Lynn and Quinn floated closer to my side. My lungs felt like they were on fire.

"Let's stop for the night," Lynn suggested as Flynn paused, turning around to look at the three of us before looking up at the sunset above.

"You're right," he agreed, moving closer and seeing how I was struggling, "I'm sorry, Love."

All three of them touched either arm, and the breath whooshed back into my lungs, the burning sensation dissipating completely.

I stared into those violet eyes, remembering the earlier conversation about his gift of sight while Quinn was the handy one. The man himself stepped away to build a fire while Lynn held onto my arm. He was the support—the extreme empath.

Nearly forgetting Flynn apologized, I tilted my head, "Why did *you* apologize?"

Lynn led me to a flat tree stump as Flynn looked off into the distance again. *Did he envision something else?*

His face turned serious, and my heart skipped a beat as he stepped away.

"I saw what *he*…what *they* did to you. *Everything.*"

Tears filled his eyes while I looked at the other guys who had their downcast looks as if they lived and saw my pain, too.

The air changed around us, and my heart split open. The fire igniting from eight feet away distracted me from the uncomfortable mood.

"I don't… I can't," I choked out, trying to bury those rushing emotions I tucked away to survive. Even if I did find a sense of peace in their presence, it wouldn't change what occurred.

"They will suffer a fate worse than death. Nelly is merciless when it comes to people important to him, and we will follow suit in our own way," Flynn mentioned quietly, kneeling before me to take my other hand.

Staring down into his caring violet eyes, Quinn appeared at my left side, leaning his head on my shoulder. Lynn was at my right.

As much as I wanted to lean away from their touch, my spirit felt comforted and safe by their gestures. My mind scrambled to explain the connection, but I came up short.

Magic couldn't be responsible for all of it, but I wondered what the hell was wrong with me and my emotional state.

I was too exhausted to battle it all out internally then, but I did *feel* it—the safety between the three of them. The care and genuineness. *The bond fluttered beneath the surface.*

"We will not judge if you need to cry it out. I can feel it," Lynn whispered in my ear.

Almost as if he commanded it, *I did.*

To my dismay, it was freeing to have permission and feel safe enough to let out the well of emotions. I surprised myself when I didn't push or pull away while they loosely held me through it all.

The triplets weren't pushy, and it allowed me to grieve properly. Perhaps their healing magic was working wonders on what was once a fragile, drugged mind. I was no longer trapped in a prison. *I could finally breathe in the freedom.*

Hours must have passed during my cry session because I opened my eyes and woke to the sun coming up. Why was I so warm and snug?

Bodies were nestled around me, a warm cocoon of limbs. *When did I fall asleep?*

I wiggled slightly out of two pairs of hands, sitting up and feeling the cold seep back in. I smiled down at the protectors beside me, *mates* I let into my heart far too quickly for any normal comfort. Did I care when I felt safer than I had in a while? *Hell no.*

"That was refreshing," Quinn said shortly later, yawning as the other guys stretched and sat up, too.

"You're comfy, Love," Flynn murmured, leaning over to kiss my cheek.

Stifling a giggle, the other two men did the same on my other cheek.

"Sorry to hinder our travels. I must've passed out from exhaustion," I apologized quietly.

"I aided in that to allow you to rest. You have been through a lot," Lynn admitted.

"That was kind of you. I appreciate it." I turned to smile at him, wholly fascinated by his magic even when he wasn't at full strength.

They helped me stand as Quinn spoke, moving away from us.

"I'll make us some breakfast over the fire. I think resting helped restore some of our energy, too," Quinn rubbed his hands together, blowing on his hands before flames erupted on a new pile of wood.

I gasped as pots, pans, and food appeared.

"You really are handy," I commented, appreciating the thoughtfulness.

I hadn't experienced magic on their level yet, and they had already done so much for me in a short amount of time.

Quinn gazed proudly at me, the corners of his mouth curling up as he began working on cooking.

"The three of you are healing to be around," I mused aloud, letting the safety I felt fully sink in as I watched Quinn cook from the tree stump.

The eggs and rice were in separate pans before being combined, and the smell of bacon wafted through the air, awakening my stomach as it growled in response.

"That's how it's supposed to feel when you're mated, although it's not a completed bond until we have sex. It's still lingering between us, a tether, but it's so much stronger once it's sealed with our bodies. We wouldn't ever pressure you into that, though," Flynn said from my right.

Sex, huh?

Appreciating their honesty, I wracked my mind, trying to recall what the books stated about mates, but I came up short. Being distracted by the men around me with their lovely eyes and sweetness didn't help.

"I didn't realize... I appreciate the clarification and patience. I'm still trying to wrap my head around having multiple mates," I exhaled slowly while letting my mind drift off, staring into the flames of the fire.

"Of course, take all the time you need." Lynn smiled, standing between Flynn and Quinn as the sun rose over the horizon, shining a light directly onto him.

What an angel of a man.

Just what would I do with all these mates? Was my heart big enough for them? Would we share each other?

Pulling me from my thoughts, Quinn handed plates of food out to each of us, and we ate the delicious breakfast he made.

I was enjoying it so much that I moaned loudly in satisfaction.

Flynn coughed as Quinn grinned. Lynn winked as I looked at my soon-to-be empty plate, apologizing. "Sorry… It's delicious, Quinn."

Embarrassed by my reaction, I avoided their gazes.

"Not a problem. Although if you're going to moan like that at us, I'd rather be filling you up with my cock, not food," Quinn admitted in return.

My cheeks heated, and I threw the small piece of meat left on my plate at him as I puffed my cheeks.

"Forgive him, Love. We'll be thinking of nothing else until the bond is completed. It's nothing personal, and we respect your boundaries. Ignore his comments. He can't seem to help himself," Flynn responded sweetly before reprimanding Quinn with a sharp glance.

I looked away from all of them; *these mates were going to be trouble, and my heart wasn't ready just yet.*

Saying nothing else, everyone finished up breakfast, and then we continued our journey.

The silence dragged on as we were nearing the city. I could make out the sirens and noise that I recalled from my first day in it. Sirap hadn't changed, but hearing the noise at a distance again made me jump, latching onto Lynn's hand.

"We've got you," he confirmed as I took a deep breath, feeling the truth laced in his words. I knew his magic was at work as my hand tingled and centered solely where he held my hand.

"Thank you," I mumbled as the city grew in loudness.

There were still cars and honks even if it wasn't as busy as it was in the central part of the city.

"There's something ahead," Flynn told us, holding his hand out to stop us in our tracks, "wait here. I'll check it out."

Quinn followed him, nodding to Lynn as the two men disappeared. The air changed again, giving rise to unease.

"Do you think everything is okay?" I asked Lynn, the anxiety sitting heavy in my stomach.

I squeezed his hand, an odd sense of foreboding overcoming me.

No.

He returned the squeeze, shrugging in response when a sudden large, dark figure appeared, a beastly-looking creature that loomed over us. My heart fell immediately. The beast was too close for my liking.

Shit.

Lynn tried to step in front of me and defend us once the beast stalked forward. Before Lynn could do anything, the beast picked him up like he weighed nothing, tossing him through one of the building windows nearby. *They didn't have their strength fully restored and couldn't protect me.*

Frantic on the inside, I tried to steel my facial expression. I was alone with the scary-looking furball in front of me. Then, it stalked toward me. No, no!

Breathe, Tom, just breathe.

As the beast approached, I realized how burly it was, hairy with black eyes and a menacing growl. I shuddered at the sound as pure dread filled me.

"You're coming with me, little girl," a deep voice boomed through my eardrums, and I didn't have it in me to fight. I was no match for the beast. My mates were nowhere to be found, and I feared for their safety.

I couldn't feel their energy in the air, and I nearly broke over it.

"Just don't hurt them anymore, and I'll go with you." My voice came out shaky while I hoped that bargaining with it would help.

The beast laughed huskily, bending down to throw me over its shoulder, and the ground seemed so far away from me. Muscle was packed under all that fur as I realized the strength it possessed. At least the creature wasn't trying to kill me *yet.*

"You already sound so obedient and submissive. *This is going to be fun, my pet.*"

I closed my eyes, trying not to shake under the promise of whatever fun he had in store for me. I stared down at the ground, the pavement moving by under my blank stare while the beast walked briskly away.

Already, I was missing the safety of my newly found mates; I bit back my tears.

I was absolutely hopeless now.

What did the beast have planned for me? Was it to return me to those grimy toads?

I tried to bite down the fear that was trying to suffocate me, a silent sob escaping. I made a vow to myself, trying to find some light in the encroaching darkness rushing to overtake my mind and body.

I'd rather die before I became a victim again.

Chapter 6

"I Stayed Because I Had To"

Chapter Playlist:
"Me and the Devil" by Soap&Skin
"Slaves" by ACTORS
"Exorcism" by Clarity
"Take Your Pleasures Sadly" by R. Missing

Tom

The collar and chain around my neck filled me with false pride as I followed him into the dark. Burk was the beast's name, and he had nothing to do with my kidnappers from before. He was *different*, consuming me as if I had no choice in the matter.

The low lighting of his dungeon called to me as I prepared to empty my mind and focus on my only duty. To submit to him.

Burk ran his own BDSM dungeon.

Another enemy of Nelly's, of course, but he was far more patient in getting one over on him than the grimy toads from before. At least he pleased me and channeled me in other ways I found useful. I was new to the BDSM world but quickly found comfort in it. It was undoubtedly a prison, but it was better than before, unlike the one of my own making. I wouldn't be a victim, so I made my choice when I bargained with the beast on the street.

The Saint Andrew's Cross on the wall pulled me from my thoughts and caused my skin to heat up. The cross *and* the spanking bench were some of my favorite activities. It was also my reward for behaving. Feeling the chain yank me slightly, I held my breath as the warmth spread throughout my entire body before settling at my core.

The restraints hung on the cross as Burk led me through the routine of strapping me in, finishing up with a tug to the chain around my neck.

His brown eyes flared to life as my mouth fell open, rejoicing in what was coming. My mouth watered as if I could almost taste it.

"You are *my* good little girl, one I'd die for. You make Daddy so happy. My perfect little submissive," he praised.

My blood flared to life as nothing else filled my mind except that praise. Burk was what I called a pleasure sadist. He made me work for it, but the reward was often worth the pain. It was healing for me as I no longer shied away from sex. Burk aided in that, being patient and understanding of the trauma in the wake of what the toads did to me.

His dominance wasn't to be trifled with, and he allowed no one to touch me but him. Grateful for it and *him,* he brought me back to the present, asking me to make my choice.

"Paddle or crop, baby girl?" His tone was low and deep, so deep I could feel it in my belly. I rubbed my bare thighs together, feeling the slickness gather at my pussy.

"Whatever you think I deserve, Sir. My pleasure is yours," I told him so obediently as I knew he loved to consume me and eat up my words of submission.

A low growl left him as he grabbed my chin between his large fingers, bringing those lips to mine, tasting his sweat and musk.

"Why not both? You are the object of all my desires, and soon I will have your very soul."

Please, take it—I don't need it.

I closed my eyes as he pulled away, not bothering to ponder what he meant by *soon.* Awaiting his return, my ears focused on his location from nearby as he grabbed the paddle and crop from the rack.

I felt the crop across my belly first. A garbled sound left me as I swallowed hard, getting my mind in the zone with each stroke against my skin.

"Let me hear you, baby," he got out before the paddle went across my cunt; my eyes shot open, and a gasped moan of need left my lips on command.

"Yes, good girl. Once you scream for me, I'll stuff you with my cock, and someday I'll breed the fuck out of you. You are *mine.* Remember that always."

The paddle went against the same spot and the crop to the back of my knee.

I cried out, the sensation of pain and incoming pleasure flooding my veins.

"What do you say to that, my dark-haired girl?"

"Yes, Daddy," I moaned loudly when he struck me across my thighs.

"That's it. So beautiful when I mark you, now, scream for Daddy," he urged on as he struck me hard on either side of me as my body obeyed. My lungs belted out the sound he asked for.

Burk was panting, removing his leather pants as the tools dropped to the floor loudly. My feet were being unlatched, and he roughly wrapped them around his waist, his cock nudging toward my center.

"You've been so good for me; it's time for me to cum all over this pussy of yours. Would you like that, pretty girl?" The desire was etched all over his face, a face that emulated dominance and masculinity.

He didn't compare to my mates, but that didn't matter when I belonged to Burk.

"Yes, Sir. *Please,"* I begged as he slammed his cock in, my head rolling back as he pounded into me until I was crumbling from cries of pleasure as he hit me deeply. I came swiftly all over him, hugging his cock tight.

He nearly howled, indicating that he was a beast down to the central core of him. My mind drifted off as he brought me into a further orgasm until I was left with nothing else. An empty bliss.

Subspace. That's what it was called during scenes of BDSM. I often fell asleep afterward, waking up to him not in bed. It stung me at first, but aftercare was something I didn't need to give myself, nor did I want it from him. Oddly enough, it was the one boundary he abided by, the only one.

Burk embodied his dominance in every facet of his nature. A mixture of beast and man. When he wasn't in beast form, he kept his dark eyes, messy brown hair, and an entire body covered in tattoos, minus his neck and face. It was initially intimidating, but I had to quickly get over it. No one messed with him, which made my situation with him more manageable.

His domain was near the city's outskirts, outside Nelly's and *Momma Toad's Trio of Terrible Sons*. My mates would never find me when I was locked away in a dungeon, but that was okay. I accepted it weeks ago. There were worse fates.

In *my* role, I was supposed to *do as he said* without question. Burk mentioned how he didn't tolerate brats, but he wouldn't harm my mates as long as I was *good*. Somehow, ultimate obeisance gave me back *my* control. I didn't need to think about anything or be anyone. *He did it for me.*

My mates were also safe; at least, I hoped they still were. Burk also confirmed my mother was alive and well. What else did I need other than him?

I didn't have time to think of my mates, and although my newest pleasure prison wasn't ideal, it kept me and the others safe. It was *my* choice to endure pain and turn it into pleasure. Weirdly, Burk gave me a gift I didn't know I was capable of. Also, he quickly found out how I responded and basked in the praise he gave me.

Lost in his dark world, I was *so good* at being submissive that I wore *his* collar as a badge of pride and honor to have him as my Dom—I fucking earned it. *Daddy's Girl.*

Maybe someday, I'd choose my own prison and be happy there. Burk wasn't too bad, even if I didn't feel anything romantically toward him–I stayed because I had to.

I didn't talk to anyone or laugh. Silent obedience was my game. It was all about pleasure—giving, receiving, and doing everything he said. The words *"good girl," and "baby girl,"* were some that awakened something deep within me. Degradation wasn't my favorite, but thankfully, Burk went with praise instead.

Learning the ropes within the dungeon had reshaped my broken mind. It was *still* broken in a different sense—I had officially given up. I learned not to fear the dark anymore, *these prisons,* or the enemies that were my own. *'Keep your enemies closer,' as the toads had said.*

I learned later that Burk disguised himself as an ordinary patron at The Parisian that first night with Nelly, and he was transfixed on taking me for himself. It was my smile and alluring red hair that captivated him.

Everything that happened to me occurred because of *one fucking night.* I had to accept being in the arms of one enemy versus another. It made everything easier to bear. I'd go insane otherwise, for had I kept my ass at home on my twenty-first birthday, none of the shit would have happened. But no, *I'm a naïve little girl who had too big of a dream to have it not come true.*

Instead, I got railed each night by a shifter-beast Dom with multiple orgasms after getting my ass spanked red or until I bruised. I was passed being fucked in the head, and my misfortunes held the only light for me to see.

One evening, months later, Burk stood at the side of the bed after scening with my favorite spanking bench and nipple clamps. My body was coasting my favorite place to be—empty subspace, after having my ass spanked red.

"Daddy needs to step away for a while for business. Will you be okay, doll?"

I hummed in response as he chuckled, petting my hair before telling me to sit up.

"Drink this down, baby. It will help you get a more restful sleep. I'll return by the time you awaken."

My eyes were closed as I opened my mouth, feeling two pills slide in as he handed me a glass of water.

"Thank you, Daddy," I told him, tucking the pills under my tongue and pretending to swallow them.

"There you go, baby girl. Let me tuck you in before I leave." He took the glass from me, setting it on the nightstand.

I murmured random pleasured sounds, appreciating his care as he tucked me in tight, kissing my forehead. Beneath my eyelids, it went even darker when he shut the light off, leaving and closing the door quietly behind him.

I was a great actress pretending to love him for my survival.

I quickly grabbed the pills out of my mouth and shoved them into the pillowcase. Counting to sixty, first, my eyes shot open as I jumped out of bed after wrestling with the tucked-in blankets.

My heart thrummed with new life and purpose as I raced into the bathroom to scrub him from my skin. The collar I always wore was placed on the pillow in the meantime. The water was scalding hot, bringing me back to present survival mode.

I could feel my body begin to fight partially of whatever he gave me by the time I stepped out from the steam to find something to wear. Some of the pills absorbed on my tongue, but not entirely, so thankfully, I wouldn't be overcome by sleep.

I was mentally making an escape plan, noting where the known exits were for the best way out. Thank goodness I had paid attention for all the months serving him.

Wiping the damp mirror, I stared into my reflection. My eyes were sunken in, and I looked *haunted*. Burk had forced me to dye my hair black months before, and it looked like I was even more petite with weight loss due to the strict diet I ate. I'm sorry, the strict diet from *my master*.

With a heavy sigh, I flicked off the light, avoiding the face in the mirror and moving to the bedroom to pull on the only black dress I owned that didn't reveal everything to the world. Throwing on the black cloak, I scribbled a note from the pen and paper in the drawer, telling him if he tried to find me, I'd have my mates kill him. *It was over.*

A lie, of course, since none of them knew where I was, but it made me feel better. I was no victim, for I was merely biding my time.

Frowning, I finally left the bedroom, making my way through the low-light hallways. Thankfully, I ran into no one on my way out. It felt like I was *too lucky* once I made it outside and ran as far away as I could.

The further away I got, the more his previous words echoed in my mind.

"*You can run from me all you want, but you are mine now, little girl. Remember that I will always find you.*"

Not a victim… I'm not a victim.

I tried to shake Burk's words of warning from the beginning after he threw me over his shoulder. Part of me knew it wouldn't make a lick of difference. He wouldn't care about my mates or the note I left him. I was only a possession to him.

Chapter 7

"Shit Happens"

Tom

I stopped running once I made it to a field, choking out a sob of relief. My knees hit the ground, overcome with grief. I tasted freedom in the fresh air. There were no more drugs or mind-numbingly following Burk around. I needed to release those pent-up emotions as a silent prayer left my lips for my enemies not to find me because I couldn't take that shit anymore.

I curled up into a ball, letting myself feel what I couldn't process before that moment. The grass beneath me, how coarse and rough it was since it was fall season. The trees were turning colors, and the air had a crisp edge to it. I wasn't a prisoner out here. *I survived.*

Eventually, my tears dried, and I lay on my back, looking up at the starry sky. It meant everything to me that I could finally see it again; I admired the twinkle and realized that my mates came from *somewhere* out there. *Mates who didn't know where the hell I was.*

A deep sigh left me before I startled at a bird's cry above with the abrupt fluttering of wings.

Straining to see, I yelped when I saw my mate, Jac, suddenly standing over me.

"I never thought I'd see you again, Tommelise," he choked out, sinking beside me and gathering me into his arms. *As if he were begging for my forgiveness.*

Thinking I was done with weeping, *I wasn't.* Jac leaned his head against mine, his shoulders shaking while we cried together. Nestled against his chest, I held him tight in return because I was afraid he'd fly away from me again if I didn't.

As if he were reading my mind, "Hang on tight. I can't risk you being stolen away again. Our witches are in their tents on the opposite side of the city. I'll take you there in the morning if that's okay. I need you all to myself."

I nodded into his neck as he lifted me. I began to wonder about *our* witches, keeping my face buried. Upon feeling a cool rush of air, I spotted black feathered wings behind us. When I imagined a bird, I didn't imagine him being *human-sized.*

Relief wasn't the right word to describe how I felt being in his arms after so long. He was a part of the puzzle to all the strings that led to the interconnecting mate bonds of *six.*

The truth was, I didn't think I'd ever see him again either. I had played a role for everyone's safety. Seeing Lynn thrown like he was a ragdoll was too much, and we didn't have much time together. *The bonds were incomplete, too.*

As always, no one could find me. Unless I was drowning in water, apparently.

I closed my eyes and enjoyed his crisp, airy scent, reminding me of the forest surrounding my childhood home, bringing me comfort, smelling like *home,* too. *Just as Nelly and our witches did.*

Off into the sky, Jac soared higher. The city was pearlescent in the distance beyond his shoulders. Despite everything, I still found it beautiful.

Then again, most nightmares began as lovely dreams.

Jac finally set me down as I realized we were at the entrance of a cave on the side of a mountain. I was so lost in the view; I didn't even know we had arrived somewhere.

It was hard to tell with the moonlight contrasting with the sharp black shadows of the cave. It didn't seem to be a deep cave, but the mouth of it was big enough to still be cozy.

After taking in our surroundings with the forest of trees stretching for what seemed like forever, I briefly wondered if I'd ever get back home.

Vivid orange eyes illuminated the shadows. Jac stood there enshrouded, minus those engaging eyes. It made me wonder if his eyes shifted depending on his form and mood.

Unsure if it was my imagination, I could've sworn dark wings stretched out, making Jac look like a dark angel.

My breath caught as he stepped forward into the moonlight, fully human. The city life and memories of the past few months were fading away behind me. All I could see was my mate, who always found me.

My eyes roved over his body. There was a strong set of shoulders that had carried me and pulled me to safety, even if I drowned in transit. A deeper appreciation for him grew along with the desire to claim him and finally feel what it was like to be bonded. With the buzzing electricity at his touch, it wasn't enough for me anymore.

A breeze kissed my skin as I ogled over the handsome male bathed in moonlight. Jac's eyes seemed to glimmer from dark to orange, a unique feat that had me aching to touch him.

"I love how you're admiring what you see. *It's yours to take, Tom,*" he whispered, pulling me closer and running his fingers through my hair.

Closing my eyes, my body warmed, humming to life with newfound energy as if a battery was being charged within me. Leaning into him, I simply enjoyed having him hold me, and we stayed like that for a while before any more words were spoken.

"Do you feel comfortable telling me about the past few months?" He asked with great hesitation as he tensed up.

Opening my eyes with a heavy sigh, I did just that.

Throughout my explanation, I pulled away and paced slowly around the mouth of the cave. He leaned against the wall in the shadows, orange eyes flaring to life. Somehow, I could feel the silent anger radiating from him, or maybe it was the grunts and growls... I knew he wasn't upset over anything I did, *I don't think,* but the situation–Burk. *The time apart.*

"I'm going to kill him if I see him anytime soon. The question is, who will kill him first out of all of us?" Murderous and strangely sensual, my core heated at his words.

Justice for the past was laced in his murderous intent. The way he got defensive over me caused me to rub my thighs together.

What is wrong with you, Tom?

"Tell me about your months?" I swallowed, my mouth feeling dry as I tried to distract myself.

I turned my back to him, gazing out at the far distance of the city sparkling with its façade of perfection. It seemed so small from my vantage point, as if it wasn't evil up close, pulling me into its dark, cruel abyss.

His low voice echoed behind me, "Well, the witches and I completed our part of the bond... So, we can find each other during trouble." Jac moved closer, so close that I could feel him behind me.

"We wanted to share that experience *with you,* but unfortunately, it didn't work out that way. Safety in numbers was a priority, and we didn't want to lose each other again." Hands rubbed my shoulders, moving down my arms over the cloak.

Jac moved to stand beside me. The warmth from him soothed my inner ache and disappointment over his words. We were constantly being separated. Before I could think of anything else, he spoke again.

"I searched for Nelly and couldn't find him, so he either left when he didn't find you or went into hiding. I found Lynn, Quinn, and Flynn beaten up near where you were taken. We went back to their tents so they could mend their wounds," he paused, reaching for my hand to interlace our fingers, "I continued searching and asking around for you and Nelly both... *Nothing. We found nothing.* No one would see us at his establishments either. He's not easily trusting. It felt like a fated defeat. We were so scared for you, Tom."

I could hear it in the cracked tone of his voice, the hopelessness settling in the words, straight to my soul. A fated defeat. That's what my last prison was. I kept going by telling myself that at least they were all alive.

"And my mother, Is she safe?" I asked quietly, uncertain if I could handle bad news if there was any.

"Yes."

Sinking into his side with relief, the breeze caressed my skin as if kissing it with apologies for the past. Shivering slightly at the coolness of it, goosebumps arose when Jac continued.

"Flynn's visions showed *that bastard beast.* I mated myself to them days after they healed completely from the beast's attack. All of us have been worried. You—"

I turned suddenly, placing my fingers against his lips to silence him. The wheels in my mind were turning. I didn't want to be reminded of Burk or Led with his brothers and mother. Although I was grateful to know my mates never gave up on me, my mind was looping on the image of the four men together. It was all I could focus on.

Desire for the bond of my mates crawled slowly up my body.

Were the guys touching each other at the same time? Who took who first? Were there pledged words or an oath?

I exhaled slowly as Jac brought his hand to his lips. Those orange eyes glittered under the moonlight.

"Shit happens, Jac," Was all I could think to say before thanking him for not giving up on me.

"I—*we*—would never give up on you, *ever.*"

My finger grazed the bottom of his lip as my eyes lingered there, too, wondering what he tasted like. What would our bond feel like once it was sealed permanently with sex?

Jac gently kissed my fingertip as if sensing what was on my mind. "It would be my honor if you kissed me."

"I'm afraid I wouldn't be able to stop," I whispered breathily, deciding to be brave and meet his handsome, inviting gaze.

Was it too soon to have him? Could I afford to delay? Did he want me sexually in return?

"That would also be more than alright, should you feel comfortable." He stepped into me, his cool scent overwhelming me, and the buzzing energy flooding my veins.

"I would love nothing more, and I can't wait any longer. There are too many risks, and I…" Taking a deep breath, my senses became overloaded with a craving unlike any other, "I don't give a fuck about anything else right now. Enough time had been wasted. These bonds are aching to unite. God, Jac, *take me.*" My words tumbled out of me.

Did I really say all of that aloud?

I'd question my mental state later. I needed to make it official with one of my mates, should I get lost in the sea of all these fucking enemies or get imprisoned again.

A grunted curse left him, "I am yours," he spoke, finally capturing my lips and pulling me tight against him.

Fuck. Yes.

His lips were warm, reminding me of how good it felt to kiss Nelly. The intense connection and familiar electrifying feeling came over me, brushing against the surface even more as Jac held me close, exploring my mouth.

Quiet moans escaped me, and I felt him cup my ass and squeeze. Enjoying the feat, I grinned against his lips.

"Strip down and let me look upon you, my feathery *mate,*" I teased and pulled away, doing the same. The cloak and dress were much too hot for what I craved. His eyes remained on me until I was standing nude. The man himself was half in the moonlight, a sexy appeal making me huff.

Briefly, feathers flickered in and out of my vision, changing before my eyes until he was fully human. *What an interesting party trick.*

Biting my lip at the sight of his cock awaiting me, he stepped into the light. Jac was breathtaking as I took him in from head to toe–*naked this time*. There were delicious muscles with chest tattoos that appeared to wrap around him toward his back as if cocooned by inked wings. It suited him, my feathery bird.

My eyes drifted downward, lingering a bit longer on his length. The sheer size of it made my mouth water as it was slightly curved, begging to fill me.

He stepped closer until he was an inch away. *"You are perfect in every way. A dream to behold."*

Swooning over my mate's words, I became breathy, wetness pooling between my thighs, "Tell me, Jac, when was the last time you were *devoured?"*

That was precisely what I planned to do.

His gaze flashed with intent, luscious need. "It's been a few days," he answered smugly, "our witches are *naughty."*

I closed my eyes, picturing the scene. Lynn in the front, Jac in the middle, and Flynn or Quinn behind Jac. The other one of them would have Jac sucking his cock. *Mmm.*

"Tell me about it in great detail sometime soon." My eyes opened slowly as I told him exactly what would happen in a few moments, "Now, I'm going to devour you, mind, body, and soul."

Before anything else occurred, I immediately sank to my knees, peeking up at him between my lashes. Then, I took his lovely cock into my mouth.

A groan echoed from above me as I licked down to the base of him, using one of my hands for assistance. My hand was small, so it didn't wrap around him, but that wouldn't deter me from getting the job done. I was purring the minute his hand went into my hair. Fondling his balls with my other hand, he tightened up, moaning above me.

The sounds of him made me wetter than I already was.

His grip on my hair tightened as his breathing became more uneven. His moans were as delicious as the cock in my mouth, fueling me further to see my intended mate fall apart at *my* touch.

The blood in my veins flared to life once more, that which I thought was dead inside me. With him in my mouth, I moaned in a way, so the vibrations were intentional, making him crumble.

"If you keep doing that, I'll fall apart right here. Come sit in my lap instead," he suggested, grabbing my hands to help me up as my lips popped off his slick cock.

I tossed him a sly smile, standing to meet him. He pulled me into his lap moments later atop his clothes. Those eyes seared into me, passion pooling as he reached down to run two fingers through my slit, causing me to gasp.

"It's only fair if I get a taste." The huskiness of his voice made me unable to resist waiting any longer.

After teasing seconds of his fingers dipped in my pussy, he withdrew them, sucking each one with a low purring noise of devoted approval.

Just fill me up already.

His hands wandered to my breasts as I sank slowly on his cock. My eyes rolled back as a gasp left my lips. Fire erupted within, blinded by the desire to complete what was fated to be. Both of us were moaning at the connection of being fully seated.

Feeling stretched and invigorated, he ran his tongue over and around my nipple, pinching the other.

"Fuck, yes," I panted, encouraging him to tease my other peak.

"You taste *divine,"* he said while I ground my hips, feeling him ease in and out.

Jac felt more incredible than anything I ever experienced before. The only way to describe the change occurring within was the feeling of being awake after a long time of being asleep. So strange and fickle, yet consuming.

"Do we need to swear oaths or anything?" I managed to ask breathily, my tits bouncing as he bit his lip, clearly enjoying the sight and feel of me.

"Not unless you want to," he murmured while fondling my chest, "After we climax, you'll feel the mate bond kick in."

Well, that won't take me too long.

Deep within, the sensation began to build from his attentive lips and fingers. Being with Jac buried deep felt so *right,* and when I warned him of my upcoming finish, he answered in calling, filling me up.

I tumbled down, crashing into bliss with a final cry. My hands scrunched through his hair as he held me tight, biting down on my breast to muffle his moan.

My world exploded sensationally.

It was unlike anything. A sense of energy that filled me to the brim; a connection and a love so pure, overtook me. There was utmost passion, desire, and absolute wonder. I could *feel* him and see myself through his eyes as I focused long and hard on the new bond molding us together, singing through my very soul.

A line, a tether—he was me, and I was him. It felt like a rush, a high without a drop.

"Wow, you are absolutely incredible, Tommelise. Thank you for *choosing me."*

His heartfelt confession caused my lips to meet his. His cock was still buried within me, softening before hardening. We groaned into each other's mouths.

Thank you for sticking around and choosing me every time, too.

I froze and looked at his handsome face, my mouth going slack in shock. Those were *not* my thoughts.

"Did you just speak to me in my mind?"

Yes.

"Holy shit!"

His low, amused chuckle reverberated at my sternum as he leaned into me, placing a sweet kiss there.

"That's a neat little *mate* trick."

"It is," he agreed, leaning back to peer into the windows of my spirit that was reawakened back to life.

"I have no words for what we just did other than praising you for all you are composed of and how much this bond means to me. *I'm sorry it took so long, Tommelise. Please, forgive me."*

Cupping his face, I leaned my forehead against his.

"We're tied together now. Hopefully, it doesn't keep any of us apart for too long this time, should some other shit happen."

His hands settled on my hips. "Winter is nearing us, and Nelly is becoming harder to track. In the morning, I must leave you to search for *our fae king* before it's too late. Our witches will find you once I send the message telepathically."

I nodded as he propped himself back and pulled me with him, his cock spearing me as I moaned loudly.

"One more round?" I suggested, licking my lips and wiggling my brow as he huffed a laugh.

Anything for you.

With a pleased smile, I showered him with kisses, riding him and savoring the intensity of our newfound connection, *our bond.* The electricity thrummed in my blood.

After we came the second time, we relaxed fully into each other's arms, breathing hard from our lovemaking. We cuddled up close, speaking leisurely with gentle caresses down our sides and arms until we fell asleep. He talked about our mates, how I should prepare myself, that my mother was alive, and how Nelly was *excellent* at keeping himself hidden if he didn't want to be found.

I had never felt so cherished and loved before, and it was incredible to share with *one* person. I couldn't even fathom my four other mates, but I wouldn't shy away from such powerful bonds.

It was finally safe to let my spirit rest and dream about a better future with all of us together without so much shit keeping us apart. I needed more time to love them properly and bask in the gift of our bonds. We wouldn't be complete or at peace until all of us were together.

Someday, Tom.

Chapter 8

"You're Next Motherfucker"

Nelly

Insanity.
That's what love felt like, and all it took was one fucking night. *One. Night.*

I listened to Buz and *waited.* I reviewed the cameras obsessively, but nothing brought her back to me fast enough. There were also visits with Tom's mother, aiding her with their small farm, and my meditation exercises. My magic was easier to control after so long unused, but there was still a calling in my blood.

Nothing eased the fucking gaping hole within.

When we raided my enemy's club, those toads were *nowhere* to be found. What I *did* discover was no Tommelise, *no exotic Fay.* She escaped them. Their mockery at me over the name made me laugh while also awakening my craving for violence. It was another tally towards their deaths, and I'd kill every last one of them.

Conflicted over the good and bad news of Tom's escape, I still asked myself, *where is she?* I ran my hands through my hair in frustration. The time would come soon enough when I'd find out *exactly* what was done—*it would be war.* Just taking what was *mine* warranted their heads on a pike.

My men and I scoured the area, not finding them, which meant they were hiding or looking for Tom, too. *Cocksuckers.*

Needing a stiff drink, I called it in and had my guys withdraw while I went to my private residence outside Sirap, hidden in the forest. I needed a new strategy. Wracking my brain over the next steps, it was hours later before Buz stormed into my house, rambling about three witches and all sorts of shit.

The witches he came across had mentioned Tommelise was *my mate.* I already knew, of course, but it was curious to hear it from him. *Why did they know, and how resourceful were they?* It was unknown to me if there were witches in rival families, but one couldn't be too careful. With how on edge I was, I wasn't in the mood to fully hear it. I didn't care about witches or anyone else unless they brought her back to me. My mind was focusing solely on *finding her. And Revenge.*

I felt like a crazed, depraved villain, seeking her out as if I deserved her.

I didn't get to the top by sitting on my ass, and it was my fault for dragging her into *my shit.* Whenever I found and discovered the extent of what my enemies put her through, *I'd remind them just who the fuck I was.* If not before then.

All this fucking technology and my mate is still missing, as if Tommelise vanished into thin air.

Please be okay, sweetheart.

I was at my wit's end as the days and nights blurred together. Enough was enough.

Against Buz's advice, I put matters into my own hands.

I dyed my hair blonde, putting in brown contacts before slipping back into their territory, just as those fuckers did. *I'd be starting with those slimy toad bastards and their bitch of a mother.*

I began picking off the brothers one by one.

One, I ran over with my car. It was not ideal, but it did the trick, and it was my lucky day. The fucker dared to walk alone outside on the sidewalk, *idiot.* The other brother, *whatever his name was,* I strung up from the ceiling with a rope, making it look like a suicide. *Almost done.*

I couldn't find Led, but I did run into their mother. No doubt the bitch was responsible for *everything.* She was more challenging to corner, so I bided my time working at their bar in the strip club.

Insider secrets mentioned how she was the brains behind their operations. They bought and sold creatures against their will and would have them dance in their main strip club on the city's south side. That bitch still had green hair and way too much fucking makeup. *She's the biggest clown of all of them. HTIC- Head Toad in Charge.* What a joke.

My imagination ran wild the longer I saw how they ran shit. Although Buz disagreed with my bloody, violent methods, we would *never* sell supernatural or human beings. It angered me, unlike anything else.

So, once eyes weren't on me, I slipped behind the scenes into the bitch's office. Ironically, it was tucked away in the club too.

I should probably move my office if it was this easy.

There was no padlock on the door. I quickly slithered into her domain like silent death. The bitch's back was turned, yelling into her phone. Her green hair was straight down her back, and she wore a short black dress. Disgusted with the woman who kidnapped my mate, I readied the same rope I used to hang one of her sons. I could've sworn I heard her *ribbit* instead of a snort into the phone.

I waited with bated breath behind her until she finished speaking, oblivious to how easily a predator could get in. The toad bitch may have taken *my* girl, but the only predator in the city *was me.*

She yelled in irritation, throwing the phone against the wall beside her, cursing. *Guess that conversation was over.*

I reached around her quickly before she could do anything else, putting her into a chokehold. I hoisted her up, dragging her partially over her desk. She kicked and flailed about as vengeance boiled my veins, needing her blood as payment.

"Tell me what the fuck you've done to my mate, and I'll give you an extra minute before I kill you anyway," I spoke directly into her ear as she fought against me.

I knew I needed to pull her away from her desk since her weapons were probably stashed there.

Her laugh came out silent since I held all her air.

"I will tell you nothing," she spat, and I gave her my maniacal laugh.

"It's you and Led left. One of you will tell me. I'll burn everything. *Don't fucking test me, you toad bitch."*

I squeezed tighter, seeing her change colors before my very eyes.

Tapping my arm, I eased up slightly.

"Fine!" She heaved a breath in, coughing while I rolled my eyes over her dramatics.

"I planned to marry her off to Led," she began as I quickly had her shoved to the wall, my hand wrapped tight around her throat, but not tight enough so she couldn't speak.

"What. Did. You. Do." Venomously glaring at the woman, I *finally* began to see the fear in her dark eyes.

"I just made her strip, that's all! I had her trained, and she brought in the money. *The Exotic Fay!"*

Narrowing my eyes, "You run this shit, don't bullshit me. *What did they do to her? And don't lie, or it will be more painful for you if you do,"* I snarled as her eyes watered, and she shook her head, clearly not wanting to divulge.

"I won't ask twice," my voice was laced with malicious intent as tears pooled in the corners of those eyes I wanted to pluck out.

"Okay, okay!" She took a deep breath, my patience wearing thin.

"They weren't the nicest to her, alright? They shared her and let others–"

"Excuse me?"

My world tilted off its axis.

"Wait, don't–"

I snapped her neck.

Volcanic energy flooded me as I slit her throat, painting a message in her blood on the walls. A nice little note.

You're next motherfucker.

A river of crimson would flow through the streets, a retribution, *a promise.*

Tearing apart her office in my blinding rage, I screamed. A scream that started low in frustration before the pain of all they had done to my mate made it grow in volume. She was still alive, but how much had they ruined her?

In the destruction I caused in the room, I managed to find my mother's necklace in the bitch's drawer. I snatched it up with a growl as I dumped her alcohol all over. I kicked her lifeless body, spitting on it. She had enough alcohol to feed the flames I intended to ignite. I grabbed bottles, dumping them all through the hallway and main room.

These bastards were always trying to take what was mine.

Time to burn it to the goddamn ground.

I began the fire in the hallway, watching it ignite in the main room. People ran out screaming as I grinned, moving to the bar. A few of her henchmen rushed me to the ground as I pulled the hidden gun at my side, shooting them.

Blood splattered as I casually got up and walked to the bar, making some explosive cocktails.

Anyone else that ran towards me, I shot. I still hadn't seen Led yet, until I heard a scream coming from the toad bitch's office. It was so loud, especially with my fae senses.

Grinning and spreading out the cocktails as the place erupted in flames, I found some matches and cigarettes stashed behind the bar. I grabbed one of each, finding a gasoline can to make sure the outside burned.

I spread it, knowing the alcohol wouldn't be enough to sustain the flames that I craved.

A body without a mind. All I could feel and see were the flames as I lit up the cigarette and tossed the match down *along with my own little spark.*

Bigger flames consumed the building. *There, much better. Enough magic for it to burn hotter.*

Inhaling the smoke in my lungs, I exhaled slowly, letting it cloud around my face. Standing near a burning building nonchalantly probably wasn't wise, but I *needed* to see it. To see my handiwork.

I heard a few explosions as sirens sounded faint in the distance. Walking away, glass blew from the windows, and a few more shrieks from passersby.

Finishing the cigarette minutes later, I wandered out of their territory aimlessly until Buz found me hours later.

"What the fuck have you done, *Nelly?*"

I shrugged, clearly not about to listen to any lectures.

"They waged war on me, so I finished it. Well, *mostly*. I'm unsure if the last son escaped the flames after discovering his mother burning. But, *he's fucking dead, too.*"

He sighed heavily, looking toward the dawning sky as if the answers were located up there.

"I waited long enough, Buz; I couldn't wait a moment more," I said definitively.

"Of course, boss; I'm sorry I failed you."

I shook my head. "Don't go there. I tried things your way, and my patience has been tested to the max. I followed your suggestions, calming my arising magic, but it's anger that has a hold of me now. I went to the source and discovered what they did to her... Now, we do things *my* way—the *bloody* way. Blood answers for their crimes against her. She was innocent in all of this. It's personal now. I'm not fucking around."

He nodded in agreement, and I also looked toward the sky for answers.

Where are you, Tommelise?

The walk back to his place inside the city's center was silent, and I showered off the blood and ash stuck to me before getting some much-needed sleep. I filled him in on all the intel over the past few weeks. His rage matched mine after I finished.

"Fuck."

I nodded in agreement as we drank whisky.

A note arrived at my club days later, indicating a meeting place between borders, *"Let's finish this."*

Yes, Led, let's finish this, fucker. I won't stop until your skull cracks open on the cement.

I told Buz to remain on standby as we gathered our best guys and stood near their border, where the last son awaited me.

"One bullet for every time you fucking touched her," I said clearly as I pulled out my gun and shot him in the leg to start us off before aiming near his chest.

Shouts resounded all around. It was no time for peace talks or, well, *anything* for that matter. As soon as my finger grazed the trigger to go for round two, shots rang out, and I was hit. *Not before I pulled the trigger again.*

The rest was a blur as I went down immediately, meeting the pavement. The world spun and tilted around me as blood seeped into the streets. Mine and whoever else's. I laughed bitterly; happy I got the first shot as those idiots stood around.

I found it harder to breathe and get air.

Groaning as pain flooded me, I felt pairs of hands dragging me from the street and violence.

"I wish you used your head more, Nelly, fuck! *Don't fucking die on me!"* Buz's brows were furrowed, scowling at me. He reminded me of my parents lecturing me as my vision blurred more and more, fading.

I huffed a laugh before I gargled blood.

"Shit!" Buz began shouting, trying to stop the bleeding.

Men scattered, shouting things off in the distance that slowly started to leave my ears, fading with more gunshots cracking through the air. I was fading fast, and I succumbed to blackness before giving any orders for safety.

Her charming smile was the last thing I saw in my mind.

Chapter 9

"Clear As the Rain, Like Starlight in My Veins"

Lynn

Ever since I first laid eyes on her, I knew we would be each other's light.

Those first couple of days were unexplainable. I could feel her worries and heartache as if they were my own. With the touch of our hands upon her wet body, we healed and saved her. She was *ours*. Flynn already knew, of course, and I sensed it via touch. That electrical feeling of the bond reaching to protect, defend, and unite.

Her beauty was unparalleled, and she was so *tiny*. Her red hair was like muted flames, soft to the touch. She appeared as if she'd break easily, but no, our fighter was so strong and *still fighting*.

I could feel the dark cloud lingering faintly when we came upon her after she left Burk's Dungeon. The darkness in her went deeper than before. She learned how to channel her pain but still felt *broken* amidst the sea of enemies.

Tom was willing to do whatever it took to stay alive, which was something I felt deep within me, too.

My brothers, or my *other selves rather,* had always kept us alive ever since we realized how awful our mother was. It was no wonder why a mate like Tom was perfect. The will to survive despite all obstacles and heartache thrown at us. She is a tiny woman, conquering the world *and my heart.*

Flynn and Quinn confirmed if anyone were to heal her heart first, it would be me out of the three of us. I had a special gift bestowed when my soul split in three. *Thanks, mother.*

It was hard to explain to outsiders how the magic worked. In our home realm, our mother ruled. There was no *king.* There was a surrogate, but that's all the man who impregnated her was. She chose him by careful breeding, finding the most powerful warlock. During the last trimester, they both fused their magic to create *thr*ee instead of one.

Then, she killed him.

My mother wasn't known for being fair and just. Quite the opposite and was, in fact, *very* controlling. Once we were of age, after years of tight schedules with magic practice and learning about her matriarchy, she tried to find us partners to create more powerful magic. All we were to her were sons to breed and continue the powerful line.

Before she could wed us off to people of her choosing, *but not more powerful than her,* we fled our home realm into the night instead of attending the ball she held at the castle. Its tall, dark, looming walls felt like a prison, sitting on top of the tallest mountain, a cliché of radiating power. We were glad to escape through a magic-made portal.

Before Sirap, Ecnarf, we ventured to other worlds, and that conniving *witch* found us in each one. It took us a while to learn to spell and protect our locations.

We were young and inexperienced with world-hopping but in Sirap? *Untraceable so far.*

We didn't remain long in the city, realizing it was too chaotic to live in, and made our way to the circus outside the city, northwest in the outskirts. All of us learned what we could about how everything was run in Sirap. Flynn's magic drew us to the city, a call of some sort. Then, his visions showed how multiple mates were nearby. It wasn't until we pulled Jac and Tom out of the river that we confirmed for certain.

Since the first run-in with Tom at the riverbank, the time apart didn't ease our wounds. Even with our magic, it was difficult to find her. In a city of supernaturals and humans, it did not surprise me that some crime lords used some sort of magical protection to *hide from magic.*

Time felt endless as we tried to find Nelly and Tom simultaneously. Our mate was violent and untrusting, winning him over would take a lot. We mated with Jac after Burk took Tom to wherever he had his lair hidden. There could be no more risks of losing each other. It was a sensational night.

Jac was in the middle, me in the front, as he took me from behind. Quinn was behind him as we created a chain connecting us. Flynn had Jac suck his cock as moans filled our large bedroom in the tent. Our bed was huge and fit multiple people comfortably.

"I wish Tom was here to experience this, but fuck, you all feel incredible," Jac groaned as our pleasure intermixed.

Basking in the stretch he bestowed on me, I muffled a pleased sound as Flynn spoke. "Agreed, but for now, eyes on me, boy. Be good and drink up my cum before I fuck you senseless."

A grunt of approval left my mate's lips as the bond took flight. Jac filled me as the world changed around me.

Everything was brighter with more purpose. The string of fate links us to the universe's atoms and the magic thrumming in my blood. Pure love and sensation saturated me. We were one, in more ways than just sex.

I could feel Jac inside me with his throbbing dick as he released, and the taste of his sweat lingered, the salt on my tongue as if I licked him. There was a sense of completion but with a droning effect of how mates were missing. We would never be complete and whole without Tom and Nelly.

It was often that we tangled together after that night. I could taste Jac as if he were there with me physically. While he went off into the city again, I lay in bed dreaming of his return until his bewitching voice filled my mind.

I found Tom. My other selves were eating when I jumped out of bed to join them upon hearing Jac's voice bounce in our minds.

Fuck, finally! Quinn.

Is she okay? Me.

Where are you? Flynn.

The three of us looked at one another, debating on rushing over or not.

Wait, don't answer that. I can see a cave. As much as we wish to see our mate, we will let you have her to yourself tonight but do warn her about what lies ahead.

Jac's laugh echoed as I shook my head at Flynn's warning.

I love my Little Doms… I will tell her how fun *you are and how sweet Lynn is.*

I made a kissing sound along the telepathic connection of the bond.

Say that to my face as I stroke your feathers and fuck you at the same time for calling me little.

Oh, Flynn, you know I adore your dirty talk.

I heard him growl in my mind and aloud.

We'll meet you tomorrow, be safe. I told Jac sweetly as the rest of my brothers said their goodbyes.

I could see Flynn working his jaw as all of us groaned inwardly. It took everything within us not to go to the cave *and watch* as Jac sealed the bond with her. There was always a *next* time.

Tom had been through so much, and while we didn't want to rush her, we needed to keep her safe from the enemies around us. If they were in a cave, that meant they were outside the city and away from rivals.

To distract ourselves, we spent the evening discussing how to go about it when we picked her up the following day. She deserved *my* kindness before they got their turns with her. My other selves were far more passionate and ruthless than I was in the bedroom *and out of it.* They were dominant in nature and had their kinks. Not that I wasn't kinky; I just wasn't on their level of dominance, which was fine.

My power to feel was too profound. All I had to do was touch, and I could make anyone feel what I wanted them to, or I'd take on their pain and heartache. Some call it extreme empathy, which isn't technically wrong.

When the next day came, we met Tommelise under the canopy of trees.

A smile stretched across her face when she saw us, reminding me of the beauty of stars being born. The universe coming into existence with all the worlds and realms, all lay within her smile.

We grabbed her hands after hugging her, teleporting to our tents, and showing her around the circus. On the tour of the place, Flynn explained what various tents held and that the busiest times were on the weekends. She gaped at the random animals going by, which included lions and tigers, then an elephant. Flynn had planned to show her around more intimately whenever their solo date came.

All of us were smirking at each other while watching her gawk around the place wondrously. We knew she hadn't seen anything like it, and it was tremendous to feel her mood shift towards the lighter side. The dark cloud I sensed over from the forest was slowly dissipating.

Hanging out with her the first day allowed us to become comfortable around each other again, and we wanted her to feel *safe.* Being near her was different that time, possibly because of Jac, or maybe she missed each of us. Tom would take turns holding our hands and flashing her sweet smile.

At the end of the day, we snuggled up in our giant bed. I held her hand while my other two counterparts snuggled closer. They were greedy already, as I was finding. *I couldn't wait either.*

The following day, after Quinn cooked us a hearty breakfast of pancakes, eggs, toast, bacon, and sausage, I asked if she wanted to venture out with me for a date *without distractions from my brothers.* She readily agreed as I kissed her cheek and snapped my fingers.

She blinked, appearing in a long, flowy, pale blue dress.

"That's convenient," she grinned, leaning in to graze my cheek with her lips.

I blushed under her gaze when she pulled away.

"Shall we?" I indicated my head towards the exit as she grabbed my arm with a giggle.

Stepping outside our humble abode, the weather was cloudy yet pleasantly warm. I led us away from the circus and tents back into the woods.

The sun would peek through the clouds every so often, creating a halo effect around Tom's dark hair. It made her appear more angelic and ethereal than she already was. Then she would smile at me, and I became a puddle over it. I missed her natural hair, but it wasn't the color that truly mattered, only my beautiful mate.

We walked for a while in the quiet of our shared silence and the crunching of leaves beneath our feet. Once we reached our destination, I turned and stopped her in her tracks. Blue eyes found my gray ones.

"You are..." No words would describe how quintessential she was with her wind-blown hair, those lingering eyes, and the perfection that stood before me.

Her gaze remained on me, focusing on my lips. *Yes, now it's my chance.*

"Can I *please* kiss you?" The *please* probably sounded desperate, but I was as eager as my brothers were.

"If you don't, I'll be kissing you," she whispered, low and sensuous, while moving closer, allowing me ample opportunity to seal our lips together as they were fated to be.

Tingles traveled from head to toe at the connection, and the bond stirred deep within, inviting us to finally complete it.

Her throaty moan was all I needed to pull her into my arms. I could feel her craving *for me.* It did wonders for my self-esteem since I was considered the *shy one.* Which was fine, I guess.

I ran my fingers through her soft, dark waves. "Do you plan to keep your dark hair or change it back to your natural red?" I wondered as we pulled away breathlessly.

"I'll keep it for now. I'm not ready to face myself or who I used to be..." Her gaze turned away, and I felt her mood begin to darken, threatening to shrink into herself.

I took her chin between my fingers, not letting it happen for long. "You are beautiful either way, Tom. Will you come swim with me?"

She looked down at her attire and then back up at me in confusion. "Like this?"

The corner of my mouth perked up. "Where's your sense of adventure, *mate?* I can easily use magic to make us dry." *Or naked.*

I was teasing her, taking her hand into mine.

"Right, of course, lead the way." She flashed another one of her smiles as I led her slightly further to a little hidden spot I had created that reminded me of the home I wished I had in my original realm. Had my mother not been so cruel.

The outdoors always called to me, so for our first time together, I wanted to show her *me.* Unveiled before us was a shallow swimming spot with a corner of light and cascading waterfalls suitable to stand underneath. However, the very same corner led to a secret cavern I crafted. In it lay stars on the ceiling of various colors. They weren't harmful, but with magic, they created such beauty.

I had them in my bedroom as a boy, a scene of the starry sky with galaxies and comets. I would often dream and find comfort there during my darkest days and lonely nights of isolation, gripped by my mother's control. My stars were entirely me, *not her.* I recreated it similarly in this new world and wanted to share that part of myself with my mate.

Tommelise gasped at the scene of the waterfall before her.

The white noise of it was soothing music to my heart as she spoke, "This is beautiful, Lynn."

Staring at her, I loved how my name sounded on those sweet lips.

"It's my special place, and I wanted to share it with you… A little piece of my magic," I admitted quietly, seeing her eyes fixate on me.

"I'm honored."

I offered a small smile, stripping off my shirt and pants until I stood naked before her.

Her gaze remained fixed on me as I walked backward in the water. I could see the desire course through her and dance in those eyes. It was all I needed for my dick to stand at attention. It was unraveling to feel her desire intermixing with mine.

"There's more to see," I told her as the sky opened above, pouring down in heavy droplets. I was already halfway in the water, waiting for her.

She made a shocked sound, getting soaked by the downpour. Blinking her eyes up at the sky, she giggled with her arms outstretched as if she'd fly away.

"It's just water; it doesn't matter the form," I mentioned when she turned back to me, dropping her arms down to her sides.

With a salacious smile, Tom stripped bare, wading in the water. Her eyes remained on me with an intent that I felt scouring my blood, searching for its other mated cell before splitting, dividing, and merging back together to create something new. The roar of the bond was making me feverous, horny. Once she was upon me, I immediately took her into my arms for another passionate kiss.

I needed her closer, to be inside her once and for all. Yet, under the rain, I found a sense of romanticism in kissing my lover while being naked in the pool of water. The sounds of the rushing waterfalls and the rain created static sounds that made me bask in the moment created solely for us. It enhanced the meaningfulness of our first time together. It would be something to reminisce about later. How perfect she looked, stalking towards me with her small hips swaying before stealing the rest of my heart through her kiss. *Such sweet dreams coming true.*

Her quiet moan brought me back from the sensation of how we were feeling, the rising emotions, the desire, and lust, along with my dick poking her.

She gasped as I picked her up, wrapping her legs around me.

"Are you ready for me, Tom? Because I've waited lifetimes for you, for your light to fill my soul like stars in the sky. To finally fulfill all my hopes and dreams of something real and eternal."

Her eyes glossed over before crushing her lips onto mine. After deepening it to taste that tongue swirling intently with my own, I teleported us into the cavern, still in the water like we never left.

It took her a moment to realize we had moved. Once she did, awareness overtook her with a gasp of awe. She pulled away, her eyes darting around and above us. The change in brightness and twinkling above drew her attention from me.

"Lynn, this is… Are those *stars?*"

I couldn't hide my answering grin as she unwrapped her legs to move away and marvel more.

"Something like that. It's magic but real… See, watch."

A small, dense red star fell from above as I held out my palm for it to land gently. The warmth of it made me smile, catching her shocked expression with a hint of disbelief.

"It won't burn you. It's just warm to the touch. Not all magic is meant to cause harm."

Walking in front of her, she stared at my palm with the little ball of light, amazed by the sight. I took her hand into mine and transferred it.

"See?"

"Amazing," was all she said as she poked it with her other hand in curiosity.

A giggle slipped from her once she realized it wouldn't harm her. Her eyes reflected the light in her hand with great wonder at how I mingled stardust and magic together without burning our skin.

"Move your hand as if you're going to toss it, and it will return," I instructed, moving behind her to help.

"Okay," she went on hesitantly.

Keeping my heartfelt smile at how precious she was, I leaned down, put my face next to hers, and cupped her arms in my hands to aid.

"One," I began.

"Two," she continued, her nervous excitement echoing through my veins.

"Three," we both finished as she lifted it with enough force that it went up back to its previous spot.

"That is… Wow, Lynn. You sure are something special."

My heart thawed at the words as I turned to take her in. How magical she looked waist-deep in the water with starlight above us, giving off an iridescent glow of flickering light. Her breasts beckoned me, the need for her overtaking all my other senses.

"You are special to me, Tommelise, and I'd very much like to show you by completing our bond."

She exhaled slowly, meeting my answer with a perfect kiss I would die for over and over again.

"Is that a, yes?" I asked, wrapping my arms around her, interrupting her eager lips.

When she didn't say anything, I trailed kisses down her jaw to her neck.

"Mmm," her sounds whirred as I paused, waiting for her permission.

"Why'd you stop?" She focused on me as I loosened my grip around her.

"I need your full permission to love you, Tommelise. I do not take what is not given freely."

Her eyes reflected the stars I created above, watering.

For a moment, there was a heaviness floating. I tucked a strand of hair behind her ear, waiting for her response.

"I…would love nothing more than to experience all of you. Give me all of your light, Lynn," she exhaled a slow breath, a long pause following, "I am yours… *My mate.*"

With her full permission, I picked her up and moved us to one of the walls, bathed in a faint, colorful sea of warmth like that above us.

She exhaled before our lips met, and I cupped her nape.

Nudging my length against her, she moaned into my mouth, her tongue sliding against mine. Her hands wrapped around my shoulders and dove into my hair. Basking in her soft touch, I eased inside, feeling her stretch around me. Her moan surprised us both as I gazed upon the stunning face of my mate while her mouth fell open at the sensation of being filled.

"You have all of me in turn, *my mate. For the honor is mine.*"

She grabbed my shoulders firmly as I paced my thrusts slow, gentle, and steady. Words failed to describe how perfectly she molded to me, how I filled her as if I was always meant to be there. Her pleasured sounds motivated me as I played with her full breasts, aching for more of my touch as they pebbled.

"Y-yes."

"I am not vicious like my brothers, Tom. I will always be sweet and gentle with you. I need you to feel my tender passion when I come for you, just as I crave to feel you tighten around me, completing our bond."

She tugged on her bottom lip, suppressing a moan as I pulled out slowly, drawing out the oncoming release. I tried to hold on and last longer, but her panting and hands in my hair were undoing me.

"I welcome it," she moaned as I sunk back in deep, pulling her down into the bond with me.

Watching her and where my dick met her warmth, I teased her with my slow strokes, returning her kisses and playful caresses.

Our lovemaking was so satisfying, like those glossy blue eyes that seared my soul, flaying me alive. Her being there and the chance of us finding her was everything to me, in this world and this lifetime.

We locked eyes when she came apart around me, filling her deeply with my essence; the bond came to full fruition. A beautiful moan left her mouth, and I joined in her symphony of treasured sounds.

I felt so much closer to her. We were fated. What my senses picked up on before with my magic didn't even compare. I saw myself through her eyes, and our joining was completed.

Please, tell me you can hear me, Lynn.

Her sweet voice in my mind made me feel as if I were *home.*

Clear as the rain, like starlight in my veins.

Tommelise giggled, hugging me tight as I buried my nose into her neck, inhaling the scent of us, our heat, and the smell of water and light.

Our first time was perfect, and I could only imagine what my other selves had in store for her.

Perhaps she'd appreciate my gentleness more in time after all of us wore her out.

Either way, destiny awaited us both.

Chapter 10

"I Can See Every Angle, Every Curve"

Chapter Playlist:
"funhouse" by MOTHICA, Kailee Morgue
"Circus" by Britney Spears
"Mirrors" by PVRIS

Flynn

My turn, mate.

Lynn completed the bond. Now, it was *my* time to shine. Thankfully, Tom was warned that Quinn and I were a little more…*intense*. We'd be separated for our first time with Tom, but after? *What would she do with Quinn and me torturing her with endless pleasure?*

Not that it was a dick-measuring contest with my other selves, but I wanted to do something *fun*.

My date with Tommelise would consist of going to the circus. Then, after hours, I'd take her to the maze of mirrors.

Flashes of visions showed me a plethora of possibilities and how all of us would be together eventually. Nelly, however, was a hard person to find, even with our combined powers. His rage went beyond my mother's, and *that* was saying something.

The past few months were grueling, making me doubt how powerful my brothers and I were.

Of course, our mates would be good at hiding from us even without bonds.

There were glimpses in some of my visions of Tommelise possibly marrying someone else and how she gets taken to a dark place *yet again.* It wouldn't be easy to reach her that time, which stumped me. *Where the hell would she go?* Images winked through my mind of Nelly bleeding on the streets, but no shootouts were occurring in the city besides Nelly storming the club and taking out Led's mother and her two sons. *A shitstorm was coming.* It was merely a matter of *when. The downside to my gift of sight.*

Taking a deep breath, I wiped the foggy mirror. After a hot shower, my violet eyes shimmered in the reflection, preparing for my first date with Tom. *Would I scare her away? Was my intended plan too much?*

Dressing comfortably and hosting the great debate within, I placed my long silver-chain necklaces on, leaving my black tunic undone while lacing up my boots. I warmed over the prospect of what lay ahead for our date, ending with her coming all over my cock. *Such devious pleasure, I can't fucking wait.*

Like my other selves, I was in great shape. I didn't work out religiously, but I had enough muscles to get me by and confidently dominate the bedroom.

Leaving the bathroom, I heard Tom in the other room giggling over something one of my brothers said. Delighted to hear her joy, I smiled to myself before my mind traveled to the images of her spread before the maze of mirrors as I fucked her.

I walked outside our fancily decorated tent. We used magic for our comfort, and I was more than okay with it. A *bigger* on-the-inside type of situation for our home. However, if someone unwarranted came in, it would appear as an empty tent.

Pulling out a cigarette, I lit it as future dark visions from before lingered in the back of my mind. Tom in a hideous wedding dress and Nelly with bullet holes.

Focus, for fuck's sake.

Exhaling the smoke and distracting myself, I watched the various circus performers frantically running around. Someone was bringing an elephant, and a couple of monkeys followed behind. Some folks carried beams and props, preparing for the series of shows in the various circus tents that afternoon.

Amused by the sight of the literal circus before me, I finished my cig before Tommelise found herself outside. My heart restarted at the sight of her bringing awareness to the rising desire within. The bond was roaring to have her. *Could I honestly wait until tonight?*

My dark-haired lover stood there in a fun little black and red dress. Fit for the circus, but not in a funny way. It was alluring more than anything. My cock practically begged to be closer.

"Are you joining the others?" I teased, drawing nearer with a smug look, realizing she had makeup and red lips. *Well, fuck.*

It took everything within me to blink away images of those red lips wrapped around my cock.

Tom narrowed her eyes, her mouth curling up, "No, but I *could...* Is it too much?"

I shook my head, admiring her legs and red shoes. She had never been to a circus before, but it was judgment-free, so no one would bat an eye.

"No, but you're making it much harder for me to make it to our party after hours..."

I kissed her cheek before she tilted her head, a muddled look. "What party?"

"The party of you and me as I fuck that red lipstick off you."

Her pupils dilated, *"Flynn!"*

I shrugged nonchalantly as she playfully swatted my arm. "Sorry, Love. You *were* warned."

Teeth appeared, tugging on that perfect bottom lip I wanted to taste.

I reached for her and ran my thumb along that very same spot, hearing her soft sigh. I smeared the crimson across her face, enjoying the sight far too much before I used magic to fix it back in place.

"Although, it will be fun to watch you squirm. I may be attentive when it comes to healing the injured and searching for you, but make note, *I'm ruthless* otherwise."

Those blue eyes watched me as I leaned in and nibbled on her lip. Her breathing hitched, and I knew instantly that teasing her all day would torture us both. Especially if she was already beginning with reactions I enjoyed. The soft sighs, eyes blazing with intent, and those thighs clenching together. *Mmm.*

Just you wait, Love.

"Shall we begin this adventure, *mate?*" I whispered in her ear before holding out my hand to her.

Seeming defeated before we even started, she took my hand, and I brought it to my lips.

"If something is ever too much for you, all you need to do is say the name *Brynn.*"

"Why that name?" She tilted her head to the side in question over the female name.

"It's a shortened name for my mother. The only name that will stop me. We don't say her full name as it's bad luck, and she's bound to find us knowing her, the dreadful woman. No one wants to hear their mother's name in these sorts of situations, so I found it to be a good safe word."

To my surprise, Tom burst out laughing.

Amused by how she kept it going and doubling over, I managed to lead her to where the lions and tigers were.

"Sorry…"

I chuckled in amusement, shaking my head. "Sure, it's funny until she splits *your* soul into three. What would *you* do with permanent versions of yourself and the separated personalities?"

Her laughter ceased immediately. Seeing her blink blankly, she made a face. "Okay, fair point."

"Good girl. Glad you get it."

Her lip twitched before she gasped as we entered the colossal animal tent.

Quickly finding our seats, we settled in for the talent ahead with tricks, hoops, jumps, and fire. Having seen the shows countless times, I mostly watched Tom enjoy it. Her eyes were flickering like the flames themselves while she *oohed* and *ahhed* at the show. As if everything the performers did was *magic.* It was quite precious.

Once it was over, we stayed behind, waiting for people to leave. I pulled her into my lap, finding it hard to resist touching her. Tom's skin was soft, and she smelled sweet and sensuous. A home I didn't know I needed in my field of dreams.

Her back was against me as I wrapped my arms around her, kissing her shoulder.

"What did you think?" I asked as she leaned further into me.

"It was incredible! Is there *more* to see? Please tell me there's more!"

Settling my hands on her thighs, I lay my head against her neck.

"Of course, Love." I lightly squeezed and felt her shift, my cock stiffening over the motions.

"Tell me, how do you want me to *claim* you?" I questioned, intending to do a round of teasing.

I breathed in deep, letting myself sink into her sugary scent.

"Let me think it over… Is there another show soon?" She turned around, placing her arms across my shoulders.

Smitten with how she straddled me, *I couldn't help myself.*

"Shortly, yes… But first," I captured her lips, enjoying how I stole the breath from her lungs.

Holding her steady, I snuck a hand under her dress, letting it settle at her hip.

"Love, looks like you left yourself bare for me. How can I resist such a gift?" I murmured against those seductive lips.

She groaned as I played with her tongue; my fingers moved to her wet warmth. *She's so ready, fuck.*

A low growl reverberated in my throat as I put up a barrier around us so no one could see or hear. I remained lip-locked with my mate until she came swiftly on my fingers. Sadly, the full extent of her orgasm was muffled by my tongue, but when I finally took her in front of the mirrors, I'd eat up every last cry.

Tom clenched around my fingers, gripping onto me tight. Groaning at my massive hard-on, I removed my fingers as she leaned her head against my shoulder, heaving a sigh. Leaning back slightly, I made sure she watched me as I casually licked my fingers.

That soft fucking sigh would be my end.

"Keep making those cute noises, and I'll fuck you where everyone can see and hear you," I warned.

Her cute smirk *almost* made me do it, but people entered the tent. I dropped the barrier, fixing her smeared red lipstick that I had messed up *again*.

"Come, let us go to the acrobatic showing."

She let out a sound of delight as I helped her up, leading the way. It was tough to hide my hard-on, but thankfully, my pants were dark enough, and the crowd outside the tent was too busy to notice.

Soon, Flynn, very soon.

Impatience was driving me up the wall.

It was finally after hours when we stood outside the indoor mirror maze. I tugged Tom's arm to stop her from entering.

"Do you trust me, Love?" I asked as she faced me, seeing the blindfold I held.

I could see her mental wheels turning. It was hard to tell whether it was fear, excitement, or *both*.

The visions had shown me her times with Burk, and it seemed I had a little pleasure masochist on my hands. Yet, the whole experience she had to endure angered me. Burk was a coward for kidnapping her with his abused guise of consent. Tom would've had a better BDSM experience *with me. The prick didn't deserve any of her forced cries.*

"There's nothing to be afraid of, Love," I added gently as she exhaled slowly with a nod. "I want to hear the words, Tommelise." My tone was stern, commanding her to utter consent, for I would not take it from her like others had.

Her eyes widened slightly, "I trust you."

"Safe word?" I added, moving closer to tie the blackout blindfold around her while remembering that she enjoyed praise.

"Brynn," she breathed out once I finished tying it, cringing slightly at hearing my mother's name, *dreadful bitch.*

"That's my good girl." I turned her around to distract myself, rubbing her arms gently, "I want *all* your attention and senses focused on *me.* Tonight is about you and me. Just us in this maze of mirrors. I don't want you to take the blindfold off until I tell you. Understood?"

"Yes, Sir."

My mouth curled up at the magical words as I leaned in, hovering my lips over hers.

"I'll lead you in, Love."

Kissing her cheek briefly, I took hold of her hands, leading her in. Whenever she needed to watch her step, I would tell her. I could feel her nervousness as her palms began to sweat. Tom's breathing became more labored, and I knew she was lost in anticipating what I was about to do to her.

My plan was simple, really. Lead her into the maze, disorient her senses, tease, and capture her.

Then, I'd fuck her hard while enjoying all the angles of us from the mirrors.

I couldn't wait.

It only took five minutes for me to walk her through to where I needed her. I dimmed the colorful lights enough so she wouldn't easily find her way out. Sultry music began to play around us.

"Okay, Love. I'm going to release your hands and step away. If you don't find your way out within two minutes, then I will chase after you. If I catch you, *game over.*"

"W-what game?" Her lip quivered as my cock strained against my pants.

"The game of hide and seek, pretty girl." I turned and kissed her lips before disappearing. *"Take off your blindfold."*

Making myself nearly invisible, I watched as she hastily removed the blindfold, letting her eyes adjust.

"How am I supposed to see anything?" She whispered to herself before taking a deep breath and glancing at the mirrors around her.

Fascinated by her loss of senses, I made sure a ticking sound ricocheted before projecting my voice from nearby that she had ninety seconds left.

I heard her curse before she became frantic, wandering through the maze and hitting one dead end after another.

"I'm going to catch you, my dear," I projected myself at different angles so she would see me, gasp, and turn the opposite direction to see my reflection again, "And then I'm going to *fuck* you."

The clock ticked again, forty-five seconds.

I heard her frustration as she tried desperately to make it out, not even getting anywhere close to the entrance or exit. I let my laugh echo as I followed her. The chase was always the fun part. *My favorite was catching.* Oh, the fun to be had when I finally caught her.

Fifteen seconds.

All I heard was, *"Shit, shit!"*

Smirking, I dimmed the lights on purpose, along with the music, once the time ran out.

Cleverly, another song started at the same time as she screamed when I appeared behind her with flashing lights. *I'm a bit theatrical—sue me.*

I grabbed her, my hand over her mouth as I grunted in her ear while she tried to put up a fight. The lights turned red all around.

"Sorry, Love. *It's my turn.* I'm not *actually* sorry, though. I've been hard all day, and you'll taste so fucking sweet."

She licked my hand, which made me laugh before she *bit* me and began to run—*I* was faster. I rather enjoyed that she wasn't giving in to me right away.

"Uh-uh," I grabbed her, turning her around and slamming her into a mirrored wall, but not hard enough to hurt her.

That pretty little mouth was agape before I crushed my lips to hers, pressing myself more against her body while making sure she could *feel* my cock.

The moan of my dreams vibrated into my mouth.

"See what you do to me, Love? *This cock that aches for you.*" I nipped at her neck, enjoying the gasp.

My hand wrapped around her throat as I leaned closer. "Let's see how wet you are for me."

Happy with what I found, I groaned into her neck once I moved my fingers to her mound.

"I fucking knew it. *My kinky, perfect girl. Are you ready to finally take this cock,* to be *mine?*"

When she didn't answer, I grabbed her jaw and forced her to look at me, and her eyes were flickering with mischief. *She was enjoying our little game far too much.*

"On your knees," I instructed, wrapping my hand in her dark locks and bringing her down. "Take it out," I continued as she quickly pulled me out effortlessly, "open that pretty little mouth for me."

Her eyes narrowed playfully as she peered up, stretching her gorgeous lips in a smile. Tom licked the precum off my tip with her *eyes on me*, taking me into her mouth.

I cursed as she licked up my thick vein.

"Fuck," I said again, grunting as she bobbed her head down on me. The cherry on top was the sight of her eyes closed, enjoying the taste. I kept my hands tangled in her locks, basking in the sensation of having those red lips wrapped around me at last.

"Look at you, Love, taking me so well. That sinful little mouth."

Her moan sent my mind spiraling as I held her head and began to fuck her mouth. Giving her more praise, I felt the back of her throat and saw her eyes water.

"Tonight, your tears are *mine.* Your every breath, every scream—all your pleasures, *mine.* The mate I waited for, haunting my dreams. Now you get to see what you do to me."

Grunting over the bliss heading my way, "Yes…swallow every last drop, Love."

After another delectable moan, it was all I needed to fill her sweet, perfect mouth. Seeing her swallow without care and licking me up, *fuck.*

Her eagerness to please and drink me down did things to me. With my jaw clenched and before she could adjust, I had her up quickly against the mirror.

Aching for a taste of her gorgeous pussy, I knelt before her, moving her leg over my shoulder, wasting no more time.

I dove in, licking her juices, humming over how her taste was absolutely perfect. She called my name breathily, and my cock was back at attention.

"You're fucking soaked, Love, *and so fucking good."*

She cried out as I began to suck her clit, using consistent suction with my lips and tongue. Tom's hands dove into my hair when she came apart, and I lapped every drop. The curse that left her lips made me look up at her.

"These mirrors make you look like a goddess. I can see every angle, every curve. *My mate is perfect."*

She relaxed against the mirror, eyes fluttering open and close. I stood, tugging her a few feet away so we could see each other at more angles. It was probably overwhelming to her *but not to me.*

At her back again, I lifted her dress to expose her tasteful cunt. I ran my hand down, grabbing it. She made a strange noise as I told her, "Keep your eyes on me in the mirror."

Kissing her neck, I caught her lustful eyes in the reflection as my pretty girl obeyed.

"Look at you, standing here with me *finally* as you were meant to be. *Tell me what you need from me, and I'll deliver it on a gold platter, Love.*"

Tugging her earlobe between my teeth, I pulled as she backed her ass into me.

She looked me over in the reflection as I released her cunt from my grip and pulled off her dress. Her body pressed into mine, rubbing her ass against where I ached. A grunt of approval escaped me as I reached around her to flick her swollen peaks.

A soft moan of yearning left her lips, "Flynn, I need you to fuck me hard in front of all these mirrors. *Complete the bond. Please.*"

I gave her my best smile. "Bend over and keep watching that mirror."

I snapped my fingers, both of us fully naked as she did what was asked. Smacking her ass hard, I eased into her, aching to fill her with all of me. Her pussy stretched as I leaned and gathered her hands to put at the base of her spine.

Seeing her blue eyes and my violet ones in the mirror motivated me to ramp it up.

Her tits bounced as I increased my pace. Muffled moans turned into strangled cries. I thrived on such music echoing from those lungs. Her mouth went slack, a shout escaping. I stared at those pleasure-filled eyes. Pumping hard and fast, I smacked her ass again.

"Keep your hands there like a good girl, and I'll let you come all over my cock. Would you like that, Love?"

"Fuck. Y-yes."

I released her hands, and she kept them there before I held her hips in place. The mirrored views were fucking glorious. I could see her dripping, the way I rammed into her, and how our grunts and moans made us delirious in pleasure. Every fucking angle.

Lost in it, I felt our climaxes building, the swell and tightening of her around me.

"I choose you as my mate, now and forever, Love," I panted as she grunted out similar words, which made me grin.

With a huffed laugh, I wrapped my hand in her hair and brought her back to me as I filled her. Our climaxing moans intermingled as I released her hair, holding her tightly to my chest.

Her eyes were closed and spent as I kissed the top of her head, feeling her relax. The rushing waters of the bond flowed through me, encompassing what I already saw in my mind.

Pulling out of her, I said, "Give me a few, then I want you riding me—*off into the sunset, of course.*"

Her stifled laugh meant everything to me as I pulled her close.

"Fuck me until I can't walk, Flynn."

Say no more, Love.

With her answering grin, I knew she heard my mental voice. I pulled her down to the ground, making use of the late hour with just us. The bond ignited my body *and my cock.* It was nearly complete. She was a dream made into reality. Our bonds were magical without using magic. We were one and the same.

I couldn't have asked for any woman more perfect. My visions showed me, drawing me to this city, but the reality couldn't compare.

Now, to make good on my promises.

Chapter 11

"It Tastes Better Because of You"

Chapter Playlist:
"This Side of Paradise" by Hayley Kiyoko
"Lady" by Noé
"Thighs" by Bryony Parker

Quinn

My lover looked at me from across the dinner table as I prepared our feast, which meant *I* would be feasting off *her*. I adored food play and wanted her decorated in all the food I made before I ate and licked her clean.

I made mashed potatoes, desserts, and hors d'oeuvres.

While I cooked, I had Tommelise clean the table and lay upon it. I sent my other selves away to look for Nelly and connect with Jac. They got their time with our girl. Now, it was *my* turn to solidify the bond.

It took everything within my power not to fuck her on the table, but I needed her wet and ready for me. She looked delectable, laying there naked on her back. Those precious eyes remained on me the entire time, which caused my cock to ache *for her*.

I casually made the food and let it cool before setting it on her. Everything was on serving trays before I was ready for them.

To keep things fun, I would have her taste test before kissing her, and I rather enjoyed the flavors of what I made on her lips.

Tom was great during it all, as I checked in occasionally since she was on the table for hours. In fact, she kept her playful mood throughout the entire time.

When the time finally arrived, I took the food off the trays and placed it on her directly. The mashed potatoes went on her gorgeous breasts as I scattered the rest.

Hearing her quiet, gentle sounds made her all the more edible.

"Hmm, what should I sample first?" I stood at the head of the table and peered into her blue eyes.

Moving around to her right shoulder, I reached down and rubbed where her nipple was covered in mashed potatoes. Bringing it to my lips, I hummed in approval.

"Tastes better, I think." I smirk while enjoying the slight squirm from her. "Careful, don't want to *make a mess*, now do we?"

I grabbed a hors d'oeuvre for myself and her as we munched.

"How's my cooking?" I asked while inspecting her body for my next treat.

"It's yummy."

"Would you like more?" My blue eyes darkened, desire overtaking me at how her eyes flickered—it told me all I needed to know.

"Yes, Sir."

Kissing her nose, I fed her more bites until she was full.

"I don't mind cold mashed potatoes," I whispered in her ear, slowly moving away, "if they're from *you.*"

Licking up her left breast, I teased while peeking up to see her biting her lip. *So, precious.*

Murmuring random noises against her skin, I cleared one breast before moving to the other.

"Best mashed potatoes ever," I told her honestly, teasing her other peak and pinching her nipple between my fingers until she finally made a more audible noise.

"That's my good girl, much better. You do like praise, right?" I asked while checking in with her.

"Ye-yes," she managed to say, gasping and biting her lip.

Licking up her body, I met her mouth along with her muffled moan.

Smirking, I broke the kiss to finish the other hors d'oeuvres, going down her delicious body. I would alternate between licking, chewing my food, returning my lips to her skin, and continuing until I reached her hips.

I had drizzled chocolate sauce over her thighs with strawberries randomly placed on her legs.

"Now, it's time for dessert. There's more for later, so I'll share a few with you first if you'd like. *Since you've been my perfect princess these few hours.*"

"Yes, Sir… *Please.*" She sounded partially out of breath but still *oh so polite and sweet.*

A sly smirk spread across my lips as I took two strawberries, dipped in chocolate from her thigh, and brought it to her lips.

"Mmm," was all she said with an angelic look of seduction.

"See? I told you it tastes better because of *you*," I purred as she chewed while I waited to give her the next one.

"Yes, Sir."

Unable to resist, I gave her the next one and made my way back to her thighs, eating the few strawberries until all I had left was the drizzled chocolate.

"Grand finale, let's see how wet you are, *mate of mine.*"

She took a deep breath before biting her bottom lip again. Encouraging me further, I stripped naked, climbing onto the table between her legs.

I licked each leg up to the knee, then gazed up to see her eyes half-lidded and softer sounds escaping from such impeccable lips. My fingers found their way to her, and at no surprise to me, a *wet* cunt.

"Perfect," I whispered before licking up the rest of the chocolate sauce.

Her sounds became louder as I moved to the other thigh, saving her pussy for last.

"Quinn."

My name on her lips took me away from the last remaining control I somehow held back for hours.

The chocolate and her pussy combined tasted distinctively better. The taste of the two had me by the dick. My own aphrodisiac. Her taste alone was enough, but the chocolate was the added dessert plate for such an intricate palate.

Flicking her clit with my tongue, I sunk a finger inside her tight channel, basking in her pleasured mewls, becoming progressively louder.

Fuck.

As a pleasure dominant, I intended to give her as many orgasms as possible. However, *not before I edged her into oblivion.*

Feeling her swell, I moved my tongue and fingers away, licking her thigh from a spot of chocolate I missed. I heard her grunt her disapproval, unable to help my smile.

"Don't tell me you're one of *those.*" She frowned as my eyes traveled up to her face, thumbing her clit.

"What was that? I didn't *hear* you." Raising my brow, my undertone promised more orgasm denial, and edging if she wasn't careful.

"N-nothing," she whined, writhing and moving her hips against me, trying to add pressure and relieve herself.

"It sounded like you had something on your mind about how *I* give pleasure. Shall I add another for you?"

She shook her head, a few pleas on her lips as I stuck another finger in. Gasping, her mouth fell open as my cock throbbed over the view of her pleasure unraveling before my eyes. *A sexy fucking sight.*

After a few pumps of my fingers, she was already swelling again, so I moved away quickly.

Tom cried out in frustration while I withdrew entirely from the table.

Her reactions were so adorable I didn't have it in me to deny her a third time.

Adjusting myself, I stood near her feet as she took me in, letting those eyes linger on my cock far longer than normal as if she was studying it as it twitched.

"Go on, take a good look."

Wrapping my hands around her ankles, I pulled her to me, so her ass was at the edge.

A startled noise slipped past her lips when I placed my hand around her throat.

"Ask *nicely,* and I'll give you what you want. Tell me what you need from me, princess." I kept my leveled, husky tone as I saw her swallow hard. Teasing her with my tip, she tried to press herself onto me more, begging for me with her body.

"Please, let me come," she began to plead, making her expression pouty, "I've been so good. Let us complete our bond as you fuck me hard on this table, *Sir."*

Well, fuck. How could I deny such sweet begging?

I pushed in, giving her an intense gaze, enjoying her garbled cry. After denying her twice, I had a feeling when she finally did come, it would shatter her entirely.

"Sit up on your elbows, Tom," I instructed as I held back a groan of my own. Her sounds came rushing out once I pressed further in.

When she did raise up, I played with her tits briefly before thrusting slower. Easing out almost entirely before plunging back in.

"Look at how well you are taking me with that wet needy cunt. So perfect for me. *You're soaking me, and it's all I ever wanted since I saw you lying under the feast I made us. My good little entree, side, and dessert."*

"Fuck me," the words escaped her mouth, and I had to angle down and claim her glorious lips, unable to stop from increasing my pace.

Singing her praises, I picked her up and took her to our giant bed. Laying her down gently, I used magic to tie her arms to each post.

"This should be more comfortable for us both," I whispered while bringing her hips up at an angle, struggling against the restraints and pleasure of hitting her deep.

"Your pussy is mine tonight, Tom, and you'll keep coming until I say you've had enough. Is that clear? You know *the* word to use if you're past your limits."

She writhed, crying out. "Y-yes, Sir!"

I felt her sweet little cunt hug my cock as she came the first time, but I kept going even amidst resistance.

"Let's see if I can get another out of you before *I* come."

Taking her breast into my mouth, I shifted myself so she was under me more. Her next orgasm snuck up faster than I expected as she cried out.

"P-please."

Whether her pleas were for more or not, I pinched her other peak before moving to her lips.

"Please, what?" I looked down into those glassy, sex-blown eyes.

There was longing and desperation as she begged. "I want to touch you, Quinn."

Without another word, her hands were freed as I claimed her mouth again, sinking my tongue inside as her hands went into my hair.

Her muffled groan drove me to pull her into my lap. Tom clung to me desperately, and I warned her I was going to come.

"Fill me up and seal our bond. I am yours," she said breathlessly as I returned a similar sentiment.

"I intend to fill you up for the rest of your life. You are mine; I am yours."

I pumped my cum inside her, holding my breath as I puffed out a long sigh with my release, stilling myself; Tom met me there in our oblivion of ecstasy. Her earlier edging had driven me equally wild, knowing it would be well worth the wait.

The bond snapped into place as if held by something more potent than magic and destiny. I knew there was only one tie left, begging to complete the entirety of our bonds. My skin was on fire over her touch, magic sizzling beneath the surface. I had to praise her immediately.

You are irresistible, Tom.

You live to torture me in all the best ways, Quinn.

Good, because I'm not done.

She gasped as I suddenly flipped her over and had her on all fours. It would be a most eventful night, and I couldn't wait to tease her via our telepathic connection.

What a perfect ass.

Her pitch changed as I began to tease her more. Those moans of hers turned unholy.

Yes, that's my good girl—scream for me.

Chapter 12

"What the Hell is This Place?"

Tom

Winter had arrived, and I found myself somewhere on the city's eastern outskirts. As I walked, I thought back to being reunited with my four mates. Nelly was in hiding, apparently.

After reuniting with Jac, it was our first night alone before I met with my witches. They took me to their circus and showed me around. Once I felt comfortable in their presence again, we completed our bond with one another. I lost count of how many orgasms they gave me.

Lynn, the precious sweetheart he was, was slow and tender in our lovemaking involving water and starlight.

He began the process of completing the mate bond before his brothers, warning me of their dominance. Not that I minded.

Flynn was a sensuous partner who positioned us in front of mirrors so we could see ourselves after a day of various show acts at the circus. I was in a chokehold over how he demonstrated just how much I affected him. The next day, I was walking funny, after all.

Quinn enjoyed eating off me as his placemat before he tied me to the bed and drove me mad with need. He gave me what Burk never did. It was all about *me.* Pleasure and praise *after* torturing me with edging.

It was amazing communicating telepathically and having all their attention focused on me. They didn't judge or ridicule me as we eased into sexual relations. Safety was their game, and they made me comfortable in every way. The first night with Jac aided the process, and I appreciated how they wanted to keep me safe.

I spent those days informing them of all the bad, terrible things. How BDSM changed and ruined me, yet it was more of the abuse of the dynamic that destroyed me than the BDSM life itself. Apparently, Burk was abusive, and that's not how a Dom should be to their Sub—*at all.* According to Quinn and Flynn, anyway.

I cried when Quinn explained it before the others rushed to comfort me. I was awestruck by the buzzing energy of the bonds and how deep and genuine they were. There was still a missing piece, the mate I craved since the beginning. *All of us were.*

Too much mind chatting with them gave me a headache, so they taught me defenses, explained how some of their powers would probably manifest within me at some point, and told me not to be alarmed by it. Magic was a gift, and so was shifting. I couldn't process that either.

Jac was still on the hunt for Nelly, and hope filled me that it would all be over soon. We'd never lose one another once *all* the bonds were completed. I couldn't for the life of me figure out why he was so hard to find. For fear of my safety, it was recommended I stay out of his territory with enemies looking for Nelly and me.

One day, my mates had gone out, and I felt pulled to see my mother. I missed her so much and I felt better knowing my mates could find me. I had left a note on one of their beds that I was seeking her out.

I was feeling overwhelmed by the changes of the past few months. The bonds were nearly complete. All I could think about was my mother and my upbringing. A breeze kissed my skin as I realized there had been a temperature drop, and the trees were nearly bare of their leaves. Somehow, I got sidetracked with my thoughts, forgetting where I was going.

Leave it to me to get fucking lost in the trees after growing up under them.

Ending in an unfamiliar area, I heaved a disappointed sigh over my decision to wander instead of asking my mates.

Did I even know where my home was anymore?

It was colder than I realized as I shivered in my flowy dress, finding a spot in a huge tree trunk alcove. I'd reach out to my mates once I rested my eyes, for I became so sluggish, unable to keep them open.

Closing them for what felt like ten minutes, I opened them, realizing I was somewhere new and warm, wrapped in a blanket in a large lounge chair.

That's weird.

Confused, I looked around the new space and saw a hearth, some stairs, and a less modern kitchen with a wood stove and a fire.

"Oh good, you're awake. Here, eat some bread. I'm sure you are hungry. I found you just in time before the blizzard came. Please call me, Miss Maus." The voice was feminine with a drawl.

How far did I wander? Where the hell was I? My mates must have been worried. Hell, *I* was worried, but *at least* I was warm.

Can any of you hear me?

When the woman handed me the bread, I quietly thanked her, feeling disappointed by the non-response of my mates.

That's what I get for getting lost and wandering like an idiot.

Observing the woman moving around, I chewed the warm bread that practically melted in my mouth. *Miss Maus* was a few inches taller than me with wider hips and bust and appeared to be a couple of decades older. It was hard to tell in the firelight of the room.

"I'm making some biscuits to take to Mr. Mol. Will you come with me?"

I swallowed the bite of bread, staring at the woman across the room as she rolled the dough.

Please, answer me. Anyone?

Anxiety wracked my nerves, "I actually need to get home to see my mother and Nelly," I told her matter-of-factly.

The intense tethering of the bonds felt faint, too distant to hold on to. Something told me not to trust her, a deep clenching in my gut, so I didn't mention my other mates. Nelly was well known enough that it should suffice as an excuse to get out of the woman's hair.

"Oh, I see. You're much too far away from your home to journey out in the snow now. As for the crime king...he is dead. Everyone knows this, child."

I frowned at the first statement, moving to get up after swallowing the rest of the bread she had given me.

Wait. Not everyone knew. I certainly *didn't.*

"He is...*dead?*" I asked in disbelief, feeling my stomach sinking and my heart pitter-patter in shock.

"Stone cold *dead...* He was found shot multiple times during a shootout with the second leading crime family. *The Toad Family,* as outsiders call them. The last remaining son was shot in the leg before they opened fire on Nelly," the woman nonchalantly responded as if everyone knew the information.

Wha-what?

My lips quivered as I fought back the truth of her words and the oncoming set of tears.

"Nelly is dead? N-no, that can't be," I whined, sinking back into the warmth where I was before I began crying hysterically.

"Oh, Tommelise, don't cry over spilled milk. Quiet down, dear."

I buried my face into the covers and let the emotions take over. What an insensitive little...

"Oh! Time is a wastin'!" I heard clinking and clanking as she did whatever she was doing.

Ignoring her, I tried my best to calm my racing thoughts and hysterics.

"Now, I know why I didn't have children…" She mumbled her words, and I was beside myself.

I needed to try again to reach out and have my remaining mates locate me.

Remaining mates.

A sinking realization overtook me of a dream I had never lived. It was supposed to be faeries *with* other mates, but that dream had died with Nelly. He was the fae in those tales I read. *I was nothing.* It would be another part of myself I'd never know or experience. That *one* night was all I had of him, along with the keepsake necklace stolen by the cruel toads.

"Alright now, I'm going to go get changed while the biscuits bake. You better be feeling better before I return so we can see Mr. Mol. Don't spoil the mood *or the biscuits.*"

Frowning, I mentioned I didn't want to see the *Mol.*

"Now, don't be ungrateful. I brought you out of the harsh elements when I could have let you die out there like your fae king. Have a little decency and respect, Tommelise," she chided.

I stood up, ready to smack her.

How dare she deem me insensitive when she was acting the same way!

"Leave me alone then!"

Scowling and scoffing, "Remember whose house you're in, dear, and remember to turn that frown upside down by the time I get back. Should you still be in this state, I'll have to put you back outside to figure it out in all that snow—miles and miles from home with no one to save you."

This little…

I glared as she turned and walked out.

My tears may have stopped over her audacity, but my rage and grief ran deep. Somehow, my happy ending was merely a dead dream now.

I stared at the door she walked out of until something shimmered in the corner of my eye, drawing my attention away. My thoughts began to race, a terrible impulse slamming into me.

A dagger. Just what I needed.

My thoughts spiraled into the blackest pit as I snatched it. Staring momentarily at the shine of the metal in the firelight, a gleam of my future.

Holding my breath, I sliced my wrists and watched the crimson flow. Releasing the held air in my lungs, I dropped the knife, letting myself feel and take full awareness of what I had done. The cuts were deep, just as I intended.

Nelly was dead, and I was *still* alive. Never complete and never whole again. The remaining part of the bond would never be filled. *Gone forever.*

I heard shouts in my mind as I sank to the ground, dirt and the hard surface bruising my knees at the impact.

Tommelise!

What happened?

Where are you?

Please, don't–.

It all went black before I could respond or wonder why they hadn't answered me before.

I'll join you soon, Nelly.

Disappointment greeted me as a familiar firelight filled my vision.

Fuck me.

"And you're awake—*again. Why did you do such a stupid thing like that to yourself?*"

"I have nothing to say to you," I talked low, void of emotion, while my eyes found the stone ceiling above. With the fire and similar cave-like dampness, I had to be underground somewhere.

The woman wouldn't understand why I did what I did, and I didn't have the energy to muster an argument. Looking down at my arms, I saw they were bandaged up.

I closed my eyes, rolling them beneath my lids. The lady wanted something from me; the only question was, *what?*

"There is a long-sleeved dress right there for you to cover that up. I made more biscuits since you've been asleep for a few days. I couldn't very well leave my home with blood on the floor that took hours to clean before I bandaged you up. I applied a healing solution to help with scarring and stop the bleeding. You should be grateful for all I've done for you rather than freeze and die outside, yet you did what you did anyway."

I didn't thank her as she rummaged around the kitchen, shaking her head. I changed clothes, not giving a single fuck that she was there. I was a husk of a shell.

There, but not really.

She should've left me to bleed out on the floor.

At least then I'd see Nelly again because, apparently, only death brings me to my mates.

"That's better. Come along; it's a long way down, and I must tell you all about the man we're visiting." Her voice dragged me out of my fucked-up thoughts.

She handed me a shawl to cover my shoulders, and I sighed quietly so she wouldn't complain about me breathing too loudly.

Miss Maus explained that Mr. Mol was a single bachelor looking for a wife. He had a lot of money, was simple in his pleasures, *and he was older—much older.*

I rolled my eyes at her back, following behind her. I refused to take interest in the man, no matter how he looked or how much money he had. *I couldn't be bought—I wouldn't.*

That lady could throw me outside all she wanted. Maybe I needed to feel the cold sting of death as I froze in the elements. It's what I deserved for getting Nelly killed because he was looking for *me.*

Spiraling into a gloom, the walk was endless, until we reached the decorated caverns and the mansion-like maze underground.

What the hell is this place?

It looked tacky and awfully decorated. The colors in the entryway didn't even match. Bright, bold, and shimmery.

Mr. Mol flaunted his wealth, that's for sure. He was probably arrogant and full of himself, too. *Just fucking great.*

"Alright, be on your best behavior, Tommelise. Answer his questions and *smile.*"

Was another bitch trying to sell me off again?

For fuck's sake. Of course, that's all I was good for.

What had my life become?

The desire to have her throw me out into the elements remained at the forefront of my mind, like a hidden dagger, the same one I slept over. Maybe I'd kill her instead.

She rapped at his grotesque eyesore set of double doors, and I waited for the grand reveal of the old man to answer the door.

A gentleman opened the door, revealing his appearance to be in his late 40s or early 50s. A silver fox of a man. His age had blessed him with gray and dark hair and a few wrinkles, but I was severely disappointed in him not looking like he was decrepit and on death's door. Somehow, irritation flooded me over the stranger who lived underground and looked the way he did.

What in the absolute fuck?

He smiled warmly at Miss Maus before turning even more gorgeous blue eyes toward me.

"Please, come in," he stated while stepping aside and eyeing me, not looking away.

Feeling unsettled and shy even, I followed the dreadful woman inside his space. The image of snapping her neck overtook my mind instead of my own death. Progress, I guess.

Mr. Mol's musky scent was strong, and I wasn't sure it was a good thing.

"Who is your friend, Miss Maus?"

She turned around with a mischievous grin, one I hadn't seen from her before.

This lady is crazy.

"I brought your favorite," she reached behind me where I had the basket, handing it to him.

I turned my head and captured the way his whole demeanor lit up.

Over biscuits?

I awkwardly looked at the woman before me as a strange glint passed over her dark eyes. *'Don't mess this up, Tommelise,' those eyes seemed to say.*

Mentally flipping her off, she spun me around to face the silver fox up close.

Oh, dear.

"Hugh, this is Tommelise. She's from *up there.*"

He frowned while biting his biscuit before groaning in delight over the taste.

"These taste perfect, Miss Maus; thank you. Now, come in further and tell me more about *up there.*"

He shook my hand after I stretched it toward him, and the two of us followed him into a sitting area equally as ugly as the rest of the mismatched place.

I've never seen something so horrendous, and I've seen a lot.

"Yes, Tommelise, tell us all about *up there, about you,*" Miss Maus urged on as they sat on a loveseat, and I found myself across from them on a chair *that didn't match. Orange leather.*

"Well, I suppose I could tell you about how the sun disappeared because winter killed everything…"

I caught their gazes as the man ate his biscuits in a way that made me question whatever attractiveness was considered.

I symbolically explained how Nelly was dead, and the sun and winter were the rival crime families. How my travels and the people I met had stained my soul in some way without differentiating good and evil.

"Oh, I do love sad tales," Miss Maus mused happily.

I frowned, wiping my eyes.

"That was beautifully delivered, Tommelise. I could listen to your stories forever," he paused, looking around and drumming his fingers before standing up. "Let me work off these biscuits and show you the entirety of my place."

He marched away, inviting us to tag along behind him.

We followed without a word.

My heart ached over the long months I somehow lived through since venturing into Sirap. I'm here for a reason, whatever the reason—I didn't care.

The remaining tour took us hours and hours with needless explanations over every room from our host— nothing matched in any other part of the place—*to no one's surprise.*

Mr. Mol had odd tastes in bright, bold, non-coordinating colors. The patterns and designs didn't make sense. So abstract that no one but him appreciated it.

"This is the last stop; it looks like a dead bird ended up down here. How it got here from *up there—no idea. Dreadful thing.*"

"A bird?" I questioned, trying to look ahead into the dimness of the path that seemed to open up into a larger cave.

Ignoring anything they said next, I walked ahead, following the draft. A dark figure lay about a hundred feet away.

Vaguely, I heard *Hugh* ask Miss Maus if he could marry me or if I intended to marry someone else. She confirmed that I wasn't, and he agreed to pay her for such a match made in heaven—*for him.*

Anger laced my veins, and she squealed in delight, his chuckle following.

Ignore them, Tom. You aren't marrying anyone. Focus.

I knelt next to the dark creature laid out at an odd angle. Familiarity struck when my bond roared.

"J-Jac?" I squeaked out, reaching to touch his bloodied feathers.

My God, what happened to you, Jac? Please wake up! Can you hear me?

I whimpered, tears stinging my eyes as I leaned toward him, trying to see if he was breathing. A short movement of his chest told me that *he was.*

Relief flooded me, but he didn't respond to my questions, which made it worse.

"I'm so sorry. All of you were looking for me, and I got you hurt. And Nelly."

I muffled my cry, realizing I was the cause of all the destruction. If only I didn't leave my home.

My emotions were being torn apart. A heaviness settled upon my shoulders and chest.

"Tommelise?" Mr. Mol asked.

Staring at Jac, tears filled my vision. Miss Maus repeated my name as I glanced in their direction before turning my attention back on my fallen mate in his large dark bird form.

"I'll be back for you, Jac. *Please don't die."* It was a quiet plea.

No one answered, and worry overtook me as I took my shawl off and laid it over him, promising silently to return as soon as possible. I'd lie my way to get back to him if needed.

So, Mr. Mol needed a wife, hmm?

Chapter 13

"It Was All For the Best"

Tom

After a few lectures from Miss Maus, I ended up agreeing to *marry The Mol.*

The decision enabled me to return to his space to tend to Jac. I even snuck down a basket of supplies, and thankfully, the guy left me alone. Hugh was eager to get married and didn't seem particularly bothered about marrying a stranger—*I was a trophy.*

Ignoring the foreboding feeling that had become of my life, I found Jac in the same spot I left him.

It had been a couple of days, so I worried immensely. *Jac, please answer me.*

There was no response as I knelt beside him.

I ran my hands over his soft feathers and checked that he was still breathing.

To my surprise, I felt a twitch underneath my fingertips as they continued down his feathered chest in gentle fascination. Having never seen him in a fully transformed state, I was mesmerized and intrigued by my unconscious mate. He looked as if he were a human dressed up in a fancy bird costume. Except I knew that it wasn't a costume. Jac was beautiful, no matter what he appeared to me as. Regret filled me over my choices and selfishness.

Still running my fingers slowly, my mind drifted. I assumed when he fell, he hit his head, and that's why it was taking him so long to wake up. *At least he was still alive*. To think, I almost abandoned all of them.

I carefully checked his legs and the wings attached to the back of his arms to see if there were any points of injury. I found a few bullet holes in his arms and cried out silently.

No wonder he crashed all the way down here. How did I not catch this before?

"Oh, Jac…"

I went for my tools in the basket and got to work. My future may be doomed with a middle-aged male, but I'd do something worthwhile and save my mate. I didn't have to continue and be a selfish asshole like I had been.

Most of the bullet holes had no bullets, but one was still in his arm. I carefully poured the solution I found in Miss Maus's cabinet over his wound before fishing out the bullet successfully with tiny metal clamps.

The only reason I knew how to help the wounded was from growing up on the farm. There were always injuries with so many animals. In fact, one of the horses got hunted by one of the hunters in the woods. My mother and I saved it.

A distressed groan rumbled from under me as I finished bandaging him up while thinking of my mother.

"I don't know if you can hear me, but please let me know where it hurts or if I missed a spot." I sighed, laying my head on his chest once I finished. I was too afraid to leave him.

Please wake up soon.

I must have dozed off because when I came to, feathers were grazing my arm in a slow motion that brought me to a heightened state of awareness of him being awake.

Finally!

Tightening my arm around him, I placed a kiss on his chest of feathers.

"You helped…y-you *saved* me," he croaked out weakly.

I placed another kiss on those soft feathers of his.

Don't talk. Rest.

I heard him sigh.

Yes ma'am.

I held back a smile over his answer before asking a question.

Did I miss any spots?

No.

"Good," I said aloud while sitting up to peer down into those orange eyes, captivating my soul. There were no brown colors present in those doleful eyes. In my misery, I felt I had let him down. I gave up on my mates, on myself.

I didn't deserve them.

I'm too weak to shift. How long have I been down here? Are you okay?

"I'm not sure. To my knowledge, a few days, but it could be longer than a week. Let me check your bandages," I responded quietly, avoiding his last question as I was tired of lying and pretending.

As I checked his dressings, I moved to straddle him, careful not to hurt him.

How… Why are you down here?

"It's a long story. Apparently, I'm to be married to Mr. Mol, and Nelly is dead. Our witches weren't responding. I thoughtlessly left looking for my childhood home, and I feel more alone than ever… Until I found *you* here."

His wounds were healing nicely as I sat back on his thighs; he frowned, grimacing as he tried to shift his body to sit up more.

Nelly isn't dead. M-Married? Tommelise—.

I placed my hand on his lower abdomen. Selfish as I may be, I did what I had to.

"I was naïve to think I could go into the city and survive. It's been one thing after another, and I'm over it. I want to see my mother and go home, but I'm trapped underground instead. It's always fucking something. I already tried to kill myself, but that dreadful woman wants money for marrying me off to The Mol for finding 'such a match'. What else was I supposed to do, Jac? Other than fucking *survive. Or die.*

Dying sounded like a good plan once I heard he was dead. I'm so fucking tired…"

I-I'm sorry, Tom. I'm glad you didn't die. I need you here. I'll get better, and we'll find Nelly and our other mates. Everything will work out. Don't give up, Tommelise—nothing is impossible.

I scoffed. He must not realize that Nelly was killed because of me, and I didn't have it in me to argue, even if the misery on his face over my misfortunes killed me.

"Enough. I don't want to hear that false positivity talk. Get some rest. I'll get you some food."

Please don't leave.

"I'll come back."

I moved to stand up, and he moved his arm to stop me.

Please. Stay.

My heart tugged at his mental plea.

"You haven't eaten since who knows when. Let me take care of you. *Please.*"

I needed to feel useful instead of the failure my life had become. Dejected, he let his arm fall gently and groaned at the impact.

"Just give me a couple of hours. This place is a labyrinth. Please rest, Jac. I need you to get better so you can leave this dreadful place."

You're coming with me.

"I don't even know how to get out. It's all so deep underground."

We'll find a way.

I didn't have the energy to rebuke him, so I moved away and bid him farewell while hesitantly leaving the area to Mr. Mol's kitchen. My mental shield went up even when I knew it was wrong to do so. I wasn't lying; I was really tired of fighting. The Mol seemed like a safe option. I didn't have to worry about putting anyone in danger.

If only I kept my ass at home like my mother said.

Thankfully, I didn't run into Hugh and was able to make some sandwiches. I grabbed some fruit and snacks, placing them all in another basket. With a soft sigh of inner defeat, I made my way slowly, letting my mind roam. Jac was trapped underground with me. He wouldn't have known if Nelly died, so he was naïve in his positivity, too. It infuriated me how Jac didn't understand the bigger picture.

Determined to help him get better so he could find a way out, I picked up my pace. When I made it back to him, his eyes were shut, and I sighed with relief.

Quietly, I sat beside him, observing while lost in thought, until he opened those gorgeous eyes.

"Thank you for coming back, Tommelise."

He sounded better already.

"Here." I reached into the basket and pulled out one of the sandwiches.

Saying nothing else, he ate it.

"How are you feeling?" I asked much later after watching him eat the fruit, too.

"Slowly but surely, I'm coming around. Thank you. Will you lay with me for a while?"

I nodded, curling back up at his side once he finished. Neither of us said anything for a while, enjoying the warmth we had to offer.

"I love you, Tommelise. Give me a chance to finally prove it."

My heart sank and leaped at his words. My inner turmoil tugged me left and right.

I love you enough to let you go because you deserve better than the damaged mate beside you.

"Tom—"

"No more, *please*. Is it not enough just to hold me here for a while? Fate had other plans for us, Jac. Don't fight with me now. Rest and find a way to leave this place."

A sigh of defeat left him.

Instead of saying I loved him, I had to push him away.

It was all for the best.

Chapter 14

"This Wedding Is Over"

Chapter Playlist:
"Seven Devils" by Florence + The Machine
"Go" by MEG MYERS
"Up In Flames" by Ruelle
"Graveyard" by Halsey

Tom

Jac reluctantly left and hopefully found a way out about a week later.

I knew he was disappointed in my decisions, and the time blew by with wedding preparations. My mate said he'd be back for me, and I had to be honest with myself, I didn't believe it but kissed him goodbye anyway.

He informed me that we couldn't hear each other because we were too far underground. Our witchy mates hadn't ignored us. They couldn't find us. Yet. They could only reply before when I attempted to end my life because Miss Maus lived slightly closer to the surface. The connection was weaker.

When it was time for the wedding, Mr. Mol had decorated his ballroom and set up a separate large room to look like a chapel…and nothing matched, *of course*. It made me nauseous to view the tackiness. The dress he picked out was even more horrid. Well, it wasn't too bad, but it wasn't *me*. It was too plain and simple for my taste. Modest with a high neck that was made of white silk flowed out down my bodice, with large, unruly ruffles. The dress was too poofy and bouncy. My makeup was too bright, and I looked odd.

I'm the biggest clown in this circus show.

With a silent laugh to myself, I stared into the mirror before walking toward the altar where people waited. Feeling like a circus act, my hair was twirled up high with a weird veil that I didn't care for.

Wanting it all to be over and done with, I sighed heavily, and that's when Nelly popped into my mind.

No, don't invade my mind now. I won't be able to do this. You're dead, don't do this to me today.

I recalled dancing in his club, the way he flirted with me, and how those green eyes sparked with mischief. As terrible as people believed him, Nelly had treated me better in those few hours than those toad bitches and that beast shifter.

Nelly claimed me, but it was also *my* choice. He felt safe and warm back then.

Now, he's dead.

I huffed a ridiculous laugh as I left the room. I found myself standing alone in the long hallway. Loud, off-tune music rang through the corridors, indicating my impending doom.

Thinking back to Nelly being warm, I remembered how he felt under my fingers, the way his scent consumed me, and how much I enjoyed his dick in my mouth. The way he feasted on me as if I were someone worthy, a delicacy to be cherished. He wanted me to keep coming back for more so he wouldn't go all the way. He cleverly reeled me in enough to crave more of him.

If only I could see him again.

Strangely, I was grateful for it back then. In hindsight, it made me sad to miss out on the complete experience of him. One night with him was enough to leave a lasting impression on me.

How naïve I was and had been throughout the journey and months since. I died, got taken, and now I'm being married off.

Yet, all I could see was *him.*

Was he haunting me now? Was this my penance for going to the city?

Is this what I deserve?

My mate, the one who got away. That died.

I walked down the aisle, looking off into space, while a guy stood between me and *Hugh.* My vision faded, and all I saw was Nelly. As if I was transported to another place, as if he wasn't dead and gone. The lingering duet echoed faintly in my mind, a spectrum of colors dancing all around me.

It was a wonder to me how obsessed I was. *How it was my fault because he was looking for me.*

My heart was torn, bleeding out on the floor at the altar I didn't need to be at.

Don't marry him, Tommelise.

I wasn't sure if I imagined it, but a lost voice echoed in my mind.

I blinked, realizing that the guy and Hugh were waiting for me to say *yes.* Or say something rather.

Suddenly, *all* eyes were on me.

"No."

Gasps and murmuring echoed all around.

"I will not marry you, and this wedding is over."

I threw the bouquet I forgot I was holding right in his face. Since they were distracted by my actions, I took the opportunity to flee down the aisle, determined to get the fuck out of that awful place.

What was I even thinking? When did I start letting people make all my decisions for me?

No, this wasn't the life I deserved.

Fuck this.

Shouts echoed my name as I sought escape from the underground labyrinth. My heart pounded, anticipation rising.

Would I make it out?

I vaguely thought I saw a bird of some sort flying way overhead in the cavern outside of The Mol's mansion, and another voice echoed. A dead voice calling my name.

I'm really losing it. Being underground has made me fucking insane and delusional.

Gunshots rang out when I followed a path with cliff-like edges, hoping it would lead outside. Until someone stood in my path.

Burk.

"I've finally found you… Did you think a note was enough to sway me away? You belong to me, Little Girl. I don't give a fuck about those so-called mates of yours."

I scowled, refusing not to back down or submit unwillingly.

This guy was delusional and took advantage of a broken woman like me.

Well, not anymore.

I made my own choices now, fuck them all.

"Get out of my way. I belong to myself, asshole."

Amused by my answer, he stalked closer as I tried to get past, careful of the ledge.

"You aren't—"

Gunshots echoed behind me, sounding closer than I'd like them to be.

Fuck, fuck!

"Move!" I pushed at him as he laughed in my face.

Hell-NO!

I brought my knee up to his balls, my fight and will to be free of all the bullshit taking over.

He cursed, trying to grab at me while muttering obscenities. Whipping around, I used the heel of my shoes and kicked him right off the ledge. It was as if magic powered me to use such strength to overpower him as he had done to me so many times before.

Watching his face as he disappeared into the dark, my mouth hung open at the realization that I sent him to his death.

I peered over the edge to make sure I wasn't hallucinating, and thankfully I wasn't. He had gone into the blackness beside the ledge.

With a quick look behind me, a newfound determination overtook me.

I began to run full speed ahead.

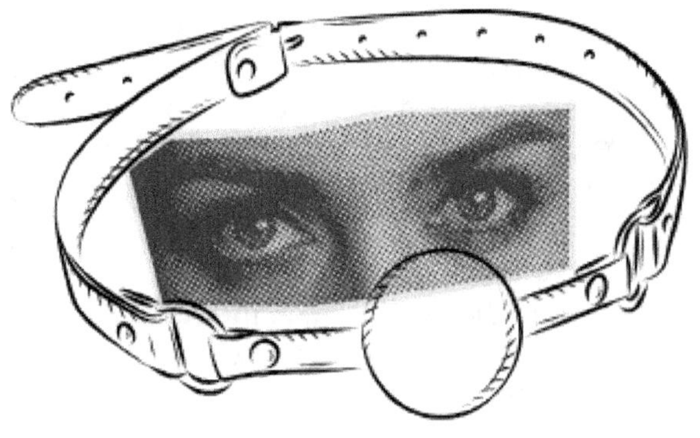

Chapter 15

"No Matter What It Takes"

Nelly

A Month Ago.

In and out of consciousness, all I saw was her face. Her smile and laughter. How it felt to be next to her. *How fucking divine she was on my tongue and lips. How good she sucked my cock.* The scent of blackberry and vanilla orchid lingered as my eyes opened to light, blinding me through the curtains.

Unsure of the time and date, I waited for awareness to settle in.

"Finally," I heard Buz's familiar voice as I groaned, feeling how the pain rippled down my spine and through my body.

"Don't move. It's been a couple of close calls. Three witches saved your life. *They claimed to know Tommelise.*"

My gaze shot toward him instantly.

Witches? Could it be who I thought it was?

"Your rash decisions of anger almost got you killed, Nel." He frowned, and realization dawned that I was in my room at my estate outside the city.

"Where are the witches now?" I asked, ignoring him.

Buz sighed in defeat. "They're on their way to check in on you. They sent a message that they had news of Tommelise. We need to talk about how we will handle things going forward."

Uh, what? Maybe I wasn't fucking hearing right.

"You told them where I live? What the fuck, Buz!"

Displeased as fuck, I held my hand up, slowly sitting and leaning against the headboard. Buz moved to help me, and I grumbled that I needed no help.

"Everyone thinks you're dead. *Including Tommelise.*"

My heart sank as I shot him a look and before I could ask him to elaborate further, a loud set of three knocks sounded far off into the house.

He left my room to answer the door without any further explanation. I needed to have a serious talk with him once I was out of bed. *Does no one fucking listen or care about safety? Or the fact that I'm in the fucking bed as a result of my own impulses?*

Buz came back quickly, waiting for my nod to let them enter.

Once I did, three males walked in as Buz introduced the dark-haired gentlemen as Flynn, Quinn, and Lynn.

Admiring their unique sets of eyes, they walked closer and bent at my side to kiss my hand.

I raised my brow at Buz, and he shrugged.

This is certainly new.

"We're glad to see you alive, Nelly." Flynn spoke as the other two nodded in agreement, his violet eyes admiring me in appreciation.

"I suppose I have you three to thank?" I tilted my head, somehow feeling calm in their presence. *Maybe I hit my head to be thinking such a thing.*

They *did* save my life... I wasn't sure how I felt about it yet.

"No thanks are necessary, but we needed to speed the healing process along since it's been over a month." Lynn spoke quietly as I looked into gray eyes that held more than one shade of gray. *Interesting.*

"What is it?" I asked, looking between them, an unsettling feeling washing over me.

Tommelise better not be hurt or so help me.

No one said anything.

"Out with it!" My irritation was growing as Flynn exhaled, slumping his shoulders and sitting at my side as if he *knew* me.

Staring at him, bewildered over his actions, his violet eyes seared mine. A strange sensation washed over me as he began. A familiar one I experienced with Tom the minute I was close enough to sense it.

His hand fell upon mine gently. "In case you didn't already know, we are intended mates. Of course, it hasn't been completed in totality, but thankfully, your cousin allowed our help and visits to save your life and keep you alive. We understand you are lost and have made this life for yourself, but our other mate needs our help. Poor Jac went missing and was found where Tommelise was taken."

Tilting my head to the side over the information, I caught Buz's leery gaze.

"Who is Jac?"

"A bird shifter and our other mate." Quinn interjected.

I rubbed my forehead with my other hand. *Mates. Plural—multiple.*

How was such a thing even possible for me?

My head began to pound, my skull expanding with all the information. *But they're not done.*

What does he mean about being lost?

"Tommelise intends to marry Hugh Mol. She thinks you are dead and has given up entirely. Our mate has suffered enough, and we need each other to bring her back home. Once and for all." Quinn continued.

"What?" I sat up more, looking toward Quinn as if I didn't hear properly while pulling my hand abruptly from Flynn.

My heart raced, thoughts overwhelming me.

Marry? A stranger? For fuck's sake.

"To succeed, we must find Jac and complete the bond with you. Unfortunately, our telepathy only reaches so far because they're deep underground. I think Hugh Mol may have a magical block down there in his fortress. I cannot be certain. We've never experienced a telepathic block unwarranted."

I stared at Flynn.

What in the absolute fuck of all fucks?

"Do you need me in here, boss?" Buz asked, no doubt feeling uncomfortable.

Waving him off, he shut the door behind him and walked away, leaving me alone with the three handsome men. *Or intended mates, rather.*

"Are the three of you triplets?" I dared to ask, ignoring all other information for the moment so I could process.

She couldn't marry someone else. Why would she ever think that was the answer? Whether I was dead or not, it shouldn't matter.

I'm a selfish man. *She's mine.*

"Yes, but *no,*" Quinn looked towards his *brothers.*

"Explain." I demanded, feeling unsettled as the nerves in my stomach swam around in anticipation.

"I'll keep it short. Our mother split our soul, that dreadful woman. We are technically the same entity, but our mother wanted more children than she had, so she split us into three. We are one and the same even though we have developed different personalities. Still, we appear similar. It's a complicated witch thing that no one but us understands." Flynn rattled on as I leaned back against the headboard again.

"So, being mated. What needs to be done? How do we find Tom? Or this Jac guy? Are you sure we're supposed to be mated?"

Amused by my questions, they went on to explain various parts of it. Tom's wedding was in a couple of weeks. We needed to keep on pretending I was dead. According to them, death was more brutal to heal from but not impossible. They were special witches with a lot of power. However, even with such power, it still took a lot of time to replenish their magic and rest themselves so they could help me.

"Has Tom completed the…*mating?*" The words tasted bitter on my tongue, but I had to know.

They nodded in response.

Fuck.

Disappointment sure was grueling.

"You are the only one left, and if you choose to complete the bonds between all of us, it keeps us connected so we can always find you—*unless you're deep underground, apparently.* It's my guess. I would assume if all of us are underground, then it works. It's very bizarre."

"The telepathy?" I questioned, trying to wrap my brain around what to do next.

Flynn nodded at my question and spoke.

"Are you open to any of it? We understand your obsession with Tom hasn't gone away. You've been holding out for her, trying to find her again. Your soul *knows* hers; you must have felt it in your blood to complete the bond. You are from the long-lost fae realm."

I raised my eyebrows at him. *Did they know I have killed? How I killed my parents for their abuse and for how they abandoned me? How I killed so many to get to where I was?*

"I need some time to think it all over. Everything fucking hurts." My aches returned as if momentarily forgotten due to the craziness of my new reality and the three men in my bedroom.

"While you think things over," Quinn stepped closer to me, "consider handing over your operation to your cousin. Work in the shadows. Keep playing dead to the world. That is the only way to keep Tom away from your many enemies."

I shot him with an accusatory look. "Are you blaming me for her suffering?"

His hands went up, and he shook his head quickly.

"We wouldn't think of blaming you." Lynn chimed in.

Looking between all of them, I exhale deeply, sadness residing deep. "I *already* blame myself. I tried to rectify it and got myself killed in the process. So, as far as I'm concerned, *I am dead.*"

They said nothing as I ruminated aloud.

"I'm not above my pride. I'd give it all up to keep her safe. I can't believe she thought marrying someone would fix her problems…even if she thought I was dead."

All three of them looked down in regret.

"She doesn't feel worthy, blames herself for everyone's misfortunes, and deems herself broken and better off without us." Lynn's tone was strained with grief.

My chest constricted over his words.

"Then we swoop in like so-called heroes and stop the wedding. After finding her location, we should complete the mating bonds and find Jac. In no particular order, of course. Whoever stops us dies. Buz can have the city. The business too. I don't care. *No matter what it takes.*"

"No matter what it takes," the three agreed in unison, giving me the chills.

It took a week for us to find our bird friend. Then, all of us solidified our bonds; when we did, it was *fucking delicious.*

I looked up at two of my mates while Jac's cock was in my mouth, and Lynn was pumping me from behind.

"Fuck, Nel, you look so fucking sexy right now." Flynn spoke as Quinn stood beside him, their violet and blue eyes lidded with seductive intent while they watched me.

You feel amazing, Lynn.

As do you, My King.

Jac let out a low rumble in warning as he shot cum down my throat, and I swallowed every drop, bathing in the delectable taste of him, *of all of them.*

Even though the three triplet witches were the same entity, they somehow tasted different. Lynn tasted like summertime and sunny-filled days. Flynn's dirty talk reminded me of why I enjoyed men, with their musk and sweat. How testosterone built these men to be handsome and strong. Quinn was the best of both brothers, offering both darkness and light.

"I'm going to come, Nelly." Lynn grunted out as I kissed Jac's inner thigh after he pulled out of my mouth, my dick hard as fuck.

As soon as Lynn filled me, Quinn knelt before me, taking my aching cock into his delicious mouth. At the same time, my moan was muffled when Flynn met my lips, conjoining our tongues into an erotic dance as I fucked Quinn's mouth. Violet eyes devoured mine.

I glanced over to see Jac and Lynn making out and I nearly came at the sight.

"You two are fucking adorable." I murmured, interrupting Flynn's kiss. The other two stole a kiss from me before resuming while Flynn took my chin.

"Eyes on me, boy."

A delightful shiver consumed me while he crashed his lips back to mine, moving his hand to my nape and squeezing. Feeling myself thicken and throb at Quinn's exquisite suction, I came hard. The stimulation was too much to bear, and goddamn, it was so fucking good.

I didn't mind Flynn and Quinn being dominant in nature. Lynn was sweet and had my heart in his hands already. Jac... I had no words for how incredible he was, how they *all* were.

All of us spent a long time getting acquainted *and* fucking. All it took was Flynn and Quinn dirty talking to have me on my knees for them. I took turns fucking and being fucked by them over the course of a week. We got so wrapped up in each other that we spent little time planning for Tommelise's rescue.

I hope we weren't too late.

We spent a couple of days planning until I confirmed that anyone who stood in our way would be *killed*. My mates sighed, not entirely judging me but more worried about Tom's safety. Not that I wasn't but I felt murderous for all the fucking time wasted because of other people keeping her from me.

I was fully healed and ready to rescue my woman—*our woman*.

When the day arrived, we suited up in all black and communicated telepathically all the way underground as Jac led the way. The mental link was a clever way to communicate and no wonder it took Jac so long to get out of the place. *It was a fucking labyrinth.*

The closer we got to *The Mol's* ugly as fuck place, we realized the wedding was happening with all the decorations. We raced against time, hoping we weren't too late.

Once we reached The Mol's residence, we searched until we heard shouts.

Frozen in place, we glanced quickly at each other as Jac changed into his large, gorgeous black bird form, soaring away to investigate.

They are calling for our mate. She's run off. Flynn.

Thank fuck!

My witches grinned at my curse before I nodded and raced toward the noise. Somehow, we got split up, and I found myself at a weird ledge-like pathway meeting that toad son of a bitch I didn't kill but had bested me instead. *Prick.*

"Alright fucker, let's dance." I stormed toward him as he charged me in rage.

The shouting crowd was getting closer as I yelled Tommelise's name, a distraction I'd pay for as we both went down into the darkness over the ledge.

Chapter 16

"Am I Dreaming?"

Chapter Playlist:
"Rosyln" by Bon Iver, St. Vincent
"Crowded Out" by Funeral Suits
"Bending Back" by Art School Girlfriend

Tom

The maze underground was filled with endless caverns, looming and suffocating, until I found a strange-looking hole with light coming in.

Nearly sobbing in relief, I ran toward the light. Desperation took hold of me as I made it to the source and out into the great outdoors.

Fucking finally.

I cursed myself once more for thinking marrying Mr. Mol was the answer. *What an idiot I am.*

Glad over my decision to flee, I stumbled down into a pile of leaves, tearing my ugly dress up in the process.

Laughing hysterically, I began to rip the dress even more, making it shorter, tugging at the ruffles and fluffiness.

There. That's better.

The sun was warm against the underground chill on my skin, and I began feeling dreamy and light. It was a vision come true to be away and out of the dark.

Standing up, I undid my hair and let it fall as I walked with purpose through the woods, hoping to find my way home once and for all.

Damn anyone that gets in my way.

Tommelise, where are you?

Jac?

I nearly cried again over the sound of his voice echoing in my head. Looking around at the trees, I wondered if he was nearby.

Yes, I'm outside and so glad you can hear me. I think Hugh had the place bespelled from anyone outside his domain unless we were down there.

I shook my head, laughing through the tears.

Of course, that dull man did. I made it outside. I'm in the woods—not sure where.

I'll find you. Don't you worry. Sing a tune? It'll help us find you.

Us?

When no one answered, nervousness hit me. Would they judge me harshly for being selfish and naïve? Did they still want anything to do with me after everything? Part of me hoped they'd forgive me for placing them on the back burner and for how I grieved Nelly's death. Maybe I needed to forgive myself for it too.

With a deep breath, I thought of which tune I wanted to sing and chose one of the karaoke songs from the night I met Nelly and had sung with him. Apparently, it was from an old movie about greasers, a label I still didn't understand, quite honestly. I still loved the music anyway.

"You're the one that I want." I began and did the melodic, *Ooh, ooh, ooh, honey.'*

Feeling silly, I wondered if I was walking in circles. Everything looked the same.

We hear that lovely voice of yours.

I heard Lynn and nearly cried.

Keep singing, love. Flynn.

Oh, Flynn, it's good to hear your voice. You too, Lynn.

Hey, what about me? Quinn.

My mates found me. They had to be closer now.

Tears prickled my eyes as I tried to keep up with the chorus.

Yes, of course, Quinn. Please find me soon. I feel like I'm walking in circles.

We're coming to you, love. Thank God, Flynn.

I kept singing as my heart burned, realizing I'd never see Nelly or hear him singing the rest of the song with me.

Finally, I made it to a gorgeous meadow after the trees cleared. It was almost as if it were made of magic. It looked so ethereal, stealing my breath away. It made me wonder if my witches had anything to do with it.

Jac landed before me, tugging me into his tight embrace, those soft feathers brushing against my limbs.

"I've missed you so much, Tom," he croaked.

Tears fell as I kissed him with all the love in my heart.

"I've missed you. I'm sorry for almost making the worst mistake of my life. I hope you can forgive me for all I put you through."

He cupped my cheek, leaning his forehead against my own.

"No forgiveness needed. You're here *now*. Do you want to see our fae king?"

I huffed a laugh. "You silly bird. He's dead and he's never coming back."

He shook his head as I stared at him before I noticed something in my periphery. I looked past Jac, seeing our three witches dressed in black, looking all the more perfect.

Releasing Jac, I moved around him to run toward them. The three of them joined me in a shared tight hold.

"It's so good to see you, love."

I kissed Flynn before moving from Lynn to Quinn.

I apologized to them for what I told Jac before and they leaned their heads against mine.

"But you didn't," Quinn mentioned quietly, "and for that, you do not need to apologize. You did, however, forget someone."

Confused, I narrowed my eyes, tilting my head in question as they went silent. They looked at me before staring *past* me.

They helped me turn around, and that's where I saw a figure leaning against a tree.

"Did you think I would leave you so easily after all this time, sweetheart?"

Time stopped moving as the light from above shone perfectly on his face.

My heart fell as hands rubbed my shoulders before lightly pushing me toward the figure. I doubted the vision of the man being in front of me.

What should've been red hair was as black as Jac's feathers, but the same green eyes burned into me, setting my soul ablaze.

Am I dreaming?

Jac spoke, "No, it's as I told you. He is *alive. Also, nothing is impossible.*"

I choked out a bitter laugh at Jac's silly slogan for motivating me, even if he was *right.*

The man himself began to walk toward me as I took a nervous step forward, slowly, one after another.

"I've been searching for you everywhere. You are a hard woman to keep within grasp, but now, no one will ever take you away from me again. *Away from us.*" He said once he was upon me with the heat of his mouth as my eyes teared up again before streaming down steadily.

I touched his face to make sure I was awake, not dreaming as more tears fell.

"It seems we both missed each other and have much to make up for." I told him quietly, my emotions spiraling as I cried silently before him.

"Yes, so it seems. Don't think I'll let you out of my sights this time—not for a second." He leaned closer, capturing my lips as I quivered beneath his touch. Closing my eyes, I was almost afraid to open them and find him gone.

I muffled my cry, wrapping my arms around him and weeping into his chest more.

"I'm here, sweetheart. I am so sorry it's taken me so long to get to you. All our enemies are dead, including that Maus for thinking she had any right to sell you to. And Mol for thinking he ever had a chance. You've made me proud. You survived all of that; I survived, and now we're here. *Finally.* Please forgive me, Tommelise."

He leaned back and licked those tears away, cupping my face. Those green eyes had quiet tears of their own. I reached up to wipe them away.

"It is you I should be asking for forgiveness. All of this…was *my fault.*"

He shook his head. *"No."*

"But—"

He silenced me with a brief kiss.

"I don't ever want to hear those words again. I'm the killer with a line of enemies and you got caught in it. I need your forgiveness as I've blamed myself for your misfortunes, Tommelise."

I protested as he cupped my face in his hands.

"I never blamed you. I thought *I* killed you because you were looking for *me.*"

He huffed a laugh, touching his forehead to mine.

"I'm the hot-headed idiot who ran into that fight. You are not a misfortune, sweetheart. I do, however, need your forgiveness for one last thing."

He looked past me before peering deep into my eyes. Before I could question him, his words echoed low. Words I felt down to my core.

"I never got to complete our bond. I need to be inside you now, little one."

My blood awakened as he ripped my horrible wedding dress clean off. A quiet noise of shock left my lips as he was upon me immediately. A hungry man was about to consume me. His lips claimed mine more urgently than before. I hurriedly kicked off the rest of what I wore.

"Fuck, I missed you, Tom." He said against my skin while I tugged at his shirt.

With the snap of his fingers, he grinned while appearing naked. Huffing a laugh, he laid me down on the soft grass.

"I plan to worship you later in front of our mates, but right now, I desperately need you wrapped around my cock, coming all over it. I need to complete this bond before I lose my fucking mind."

The sound of his plea had me opening myself, his dick teasing my entrance.

"Fuck, you're so wet for me, little one. Even after all this time… Are you ready?"

With an eager nod, my gasp mingled with his moan, and his cock filled me, stretching me so wonderfully my eyes rolled back.

Then, it was my turn to curse as he finally claimed me as I wanted the entire time. No skin surface went untouched as he moved us, so I rode him in a sitting position.

My hands went into his dark locks as he did the same, locking our lips. I could feel my orgasm rushing toward me as the man trembled under me. Our souls sang loudly for the final claiming, the bond vibrating our bloodstream.

"I've waited a lifetime for someone like you, sweetheart. We'll never be torn apart again. I'll accept the entirety of the beautiful woman before me and the love you choose to give. Our bond of forever. My last missing piece."

I cried out, "Y-yes, you and me, Nelly. Give me all of you, every shadowy part."

He slammed his lips against mine as my pussy strangled his cock. When we both came with our loud shouts, I felt all sorts of strange sensations aside from the burning of the bond within.

For one, my back was burning, and when I looked into his eyes, those green eyes were embers. Nelly's ears were no longer scarred or human in appearance but were *pointed*.

I found myself touching my ears, gasping in shock at how they were pointed. Was it because the mating bonds were now complete?

As if that wasn't enough, his hair was back to its red color, and dark, black, feathery wings were spread out wide behind him. Such dark and lovely wings.

"Nelly." I whispered in awe, stroking the top of his feathers as his eyes squinted closed, roaring as he came again.

I gasped, moaning as pumped me full of his cum.

"Fuck, touching me there does things to me. Who knew I had wings?"

His laugh was bitter as I cupped his face, feeling myself heat up again in my lover's arms.

"I've never seen a more perfect fae in my life. You have matching wings, sweetheart. It means our bonds are complete."

Our eyes watered as a vision in my mind flashed of what I looked like through his eyes.

"Wow, *incredible*. Sex with you has me sprouting wings." I teased as I angled my hips, horny as hell even after finishing.

His laugh was all I needed and more.

"Now that all of us are complete, our mates want to watch." His eyes held sparks as he looked past me, and I moaned as I pushed him down to the grass.

With his wings splayed out beside us, I steadied myself, riding him as our mates moved around us to watch.

"I feel like I'm looking at a masterpiece," Lynn whispered.

"What a glorious sight, straight from a porn book." Flynn added as Quinn followed with, "I can't wait to ruffle both of your feathers."

Nelly and I huffed a laugh in between our grunts.

"Absolutely beautiful." Jac finished in wonder.

Encouraged by my mates watching, Nelly toyed with my swollen breasts as my wings fluttered behind me. Entranced by the man inside me, I came again with a loud cry.

"One more, love." Flynn responded moments after moving behind me while Quinn kneeled at Nelly's head.

Wondering what they meant, I felt the stroke of a sensitive spot on my inner wing.

It was then that Nelly joined me in an orgasm, so powerful stars speckled my vision before my eyes rolled to the back of my damn skull.

Evil.

I agree with her.

We opened our eyes and found them all grinning.

"Oh, we are going to have fun with you both." They promised.

Nelly and I exchanged a look that said there was nothing better than being tortured by the people we loved most.

Chapter 17

"That's Our Good Girl"

Chapter Playlist:
"Hurricane" by Cannons
"11:11 (Stripped Down) by Amanati, Luna Blake
"Daydreams" by Tempers

Tom

"Okay, open your eyes, Tommelise." Flynn pulled the blindfold off, but not before letting the snap of my garter echo.

Biting back my smile, I opened my eyes to the sexy dungeon around me.

A magical dungeon… You shouldn't have.

Their laughs echoed off the walls of the room.

"You witches and your magic." Nelly joked, looking at our mates.

"Flynn and I worked hard in here, with a little help from our Jac."

The man himself bowed, his leather pants tight around his groin, making me bite my lip.

Around the vast room, there was every fantasy I could think of, everything from bondage areas with a rope wall, suspension spots to the Saint Andrew's Cross, a spanking bench, a medical table, a massive cage with pillows, then a large poster bed on the other side of the room, and a considerable display of crops, paddles, tools I didn't know the name of, and costumes plus chokers.

You went all out.

They beamed at my response. I waited until they turned around to admire the room with the sensuous dim lighting before I was on my knees in a submissive pose. My eyes were down to the floor, my hands on my knees, and my back straight.

"Fuck me. Look at her, guys." Flynn spoke with a hint of amazement and pure adoration.

"Look how she kneels for us, *her mates.*" Quinn added.

"Where should we take her first?" Jac asked as Nelly disappeared and reappeared, kneeling at my side.

Feeling his hot breath, I tried to calm my racing heart and anticipation of what they'd do.

Through my mind, I saw a black collar with the word *mate* written in diamonds.

"The only men who will own your soul *and cunt.*" Nelly whispered before securing the collar around my throat.

"Look up at me, pretty girl." Flynn's tone of voice made me shiver.

When I did, he gave me the praise I longed to hear.

"You always were a good girl...*our* good girl." he continued.

"Come on, princess." Quinn held out his hand while Nelly kissed my right cheek and Jac kissed my left. Lynn was behind me, helping me up in unison with Quinn.

"Who wants to go in the cage while I tie her up so we can watch each other?" Flynn asked, rubbing his hands together in delight.

Hiding my smile, I followed him to where ropes dangled down from a suspension bar in the high ceiling. He had my arms quickly tied and stretched into an X shape.

"You look beautiful, sweetheart." Nelly's seductive whisper echoed low in my ear and my pussy. He traced his fingers over my body.

After closing and opening my eyes at how fucking good his touch felt, I looked at the cage before me.

Lynn knelt in front of Jac on all fours. Quinn locked them in with a wink as their clothes disappeared.

Flynn was kneeling before me, taking off my garter with a familiar intent of future torture.

"Grab the paddle, Quinn." He instructed.

My eyes traveled from Flynn's face so close to my wet pussy toward the cage where Jac was eating out Lynn's ass.

Nelly licked up my neck, "They look so fuckable in that cage, don't they?"

I sighed, leaning into him before I felt the brutal sting of the paddle.

"Answer him, love."

"Y-yes." I managed to get out as Flynn lifted a leg and brought his sinful tongue to where I ached the most.

He hummed in approval.

"Taste good, brother?" Quinn asked in amusement while lightly tapping my thigh before bringing the paddle across my ass again.

Mmhmm.

Nelly kneeled behind me, assaulting my rear with his tongue too. As if that weren't enough stimulation, Quinn was at my side, beginning to lick my left breast. His tongue teased my raised peak, toying with me in the best of ways after tossing the paddle to the side.

Come for them, Tom. Jac's eyes were on me then as I let my head lop to the side as I came so quickly, I wondered where I missed the rising sensation.

Fuck, you taste so fucking good, love.

Hell yeah, you do, little one. This ass is mine.

"Switch with me, Flynn. Let Nel and I stuff her while you stuff Jac.

"I like the way you think." He winked before disappearing into the cage.

The males in the cage were too much with how sexy they were. Nelly and Quinn spat on their dicks as I watched the scene unfolding in the cage.

Lynn was still kneeling on all fours as Jac eased himself inside, then Flynn prepared him while fisting his cock.

Fuck me, that's hot, seeing all my men enjoying each other.

They agreed with various grunts and sounds.

"You first, Nel." Quinn whispered before licking from my pussy all the way up to my neck.

"Relax your ass, little one." He coaxed while Quinn asked if my bound arms were still okay.

"Yes, don't fucking stop." I moaned out as Nelly eased his cock into my tight ass.

They chuckled low before leaning over my shoulder to steal a kiss from one another.

Finding the gesture sweet, I fell into the sensation of Nelly stretching me far and wide as Quinn reached around and smacked his ass.

"Mmm." Quinn told him.

Quinn lifted my leg slightly, easing himself into my already weeping cunt.

The strangled cry that left me was *ungodly* as they took turns easing in and out of me before pounding relentlessly as steady, unholy, garbled sounds left me. I could feel them both inside, and my soul withdrew from my body with how intense it was. I wondered how I'd ever come back down from the high.

"You're taking us so well, princess. I can feel you on the brink and Nel inside you."

"The closest to heaven we'll get." Nelly agreed as I spiraled into praise and sensation, nearly screaming.

"That's our good girl." I heard Flynn encourage from next to me, completely forgetting about our other mates in the cage.

Images of their previous lovemaking flashed into my mind. Jac was behind Quinn, while Lynn moved behind Nelly.

When I finally heard the groans from Quinn and Nelly, I let go, crashing around their cocks, squeezing them tight.

"Such a perfect song from our mate's lips." Flynn mused as I rode out the entirety of my orgasm.

When I finally came down from the clouds, his lips met mine, untying my hands.

My mates were intense in their sexual love as I whimpered, hearing Nelly and Quinn release rich sounds of pleasure that were enough to make me blush. I enjoyed all they had to offer and more.

Awareness of everything around me disappeared, at least until I felt myself being carried off to the bed in the room.

"You did so well. I'm proud of you, love. Rest here with me."

I didn't even have the energy to thank him as he laid me down on the mattress. After scooting in beside me, Flynn played with my hair and tucked his arm under my neck. Curling into his chest and enjoying the aftercare, I passed out, and when I came to, at who knows what time, I was engulfed in warmth.

When I woke, Flynn was behind me tucked against my backside and Nelly's thigh, as I was between Nelly's legs, laying on him and Quinn, who was in front of me. Lynn was hugging my legs as Jac curled up behind Flynn.

Smiling to myself, I lay there, feeling so loved and cherished by my gorgeous, *magical* men who made my wings take flight, completing my lifelong dream. It wasn't a storybook I read anymore, but a reality far better than I could ever hope for. No longer would we be separated and nothing stood against us. After all we had gone through, I felt we deserved happiness and sexual bliss.

The only thing that would tear us apart was being away from one another in enemy territory or the witches' mother.

She would *not* be splitting my soul. The triplets relayed that we were safe and had nothing to fear. The power of three plus their mates was far greater than one powerful witch.

Nelly gave up his throne in the city, putting his cousin in charge. Since the other enemies were eliminated, Buz didn't have too many issues and worked on cleaning up the city of crime. Old enemies of the city that trickled from older crime families tried to come out of the woodwork, but we shut them down.

I finally saw my mother and introduced her to my lovers, and we cried together during our reunion. My mother approved of Nelly after that, along with the others.

It had been so long away from home that it felt like a distant dream. Instead of a wedding in the backyard, we had a celebration of mates and being reunited. It was a celebration of love and a toast to the future.

We all wore white as we toasted and drank until the late hours. I had never seen my mother so happy in my entire life.

Life had improved after my adventures of misfortune but thankfully, they led me back to where I belonged.

In the sanctuary of my mates.

The End

A familiar tune came from the echoing speakers of a massive home hidden away from civilization. Tommelise lounged around the large house with her mates. Nelly moved to grab Tom's hand to sing and dance to their nostalgic tune.

"Do you still remember the words?" He asked with a hidden smile, clasping a necklace around her, one Tommelise had long forgotten that matched Nelly's eyes.

"I do." The light reached her blue eyes and her fond smile.

He wrapped his arm around her and took her hand into the other as they slowly danced in front of their amused mates.

They began singing the lyrics, *'You're the One That I Want.'*

Finally, Tommelise had her fae king to complete the lyrics, along with all the love and adoration from the other males who loved with every atom of their bonds.

Nelly was dead to the world outside his inner circle but was very much alive to Tom. The two and their mates made up for lost time between sinking in and out of each other and spending solo time.

So, they danced and sang, living happily with each other in seclusion with their other mates—their own kind of happily ever after, one that made sense to them as they loved each other better than anyone else could, bound and sealed by fate greater than themselves.

Neither of them could complain, though, for being loved and loving in return—in multifaceted ways, is the greatest gift of all.

Acknowledgments

Hello Preylings.

This project came about from the Fairytales Reloaded Anthology, *Down in Grimm's Dungeon*, in November 2023.

I loved working with everyone, and I'm glad some lovely authors convinced me to have Tommelise as its own standalone after the project concluded!

Anyway, time to sing praises for YOU, the reader who picked up this book!

Let's start with my beta readers and ARC readers!

I'd be lost without you, and your insight is so valuable to the editing process! You remind me how editing is a fluid process, even if it's messy.

For the ARC readers, *my cheerleaders*, I also can't do any of this without you! All of you remind me why I do this and thank you for sticking with me as I grow through each book. I love you all so dearly! ♥

To Colby, for another awesome cover! I love your face!

Last but certainly not least, to *you*, the new reader! No matter how you came across this read, thank you! I'm so happy you stuck around!

Should you decide, there's plenty of other shenanigans in the backlog which is displayed on the next page.

Xoxo

Other Books

About the Author

R.N. Arcadia is a neurodivergent, day-dreaming Pisces. They live in New Jersey with her family.

When R.N. isn't writing or working, they enjoy traveling, going to the beach, binge-watching/binge-reading whatever series they find themselves engrossed in, and listening to all sorts of music to stay sane.

https://linktr.ee/r.n.arcadia

Message From the Author

While your mental health is important, remember that authors are people who bleed and cry onto the pages to create stories. Whether you like the books, writing, scenes, or not, that is perfectly okay, but please be aware of how harmful your words can be to others. Not just for me specifically as a person, but other authors and readers too.

The world needs more kindness and empathy, not hate and assumptions.

If you ever need to address a situation or something you deem hurtful, please address it directly. I am a person just like you who is learning and growing and doesn't always get it right.

Please note that this author doesn't support the following: homophobia, transphobia, anti-LGBTQIA+, misogyny, racism, abuse, genocide, anti-mental health, and violence.

I'm sure there's more, but those are the important ones.

Mental health is real, and so are varying diagnoses.

Don't be the reason someone gives up on their dreams because you want to be a prick, or yuck someone else's yum!

That's all folks!

With love, R.N. Arcadia

www.ingramcontent.com/pod-product-compliance
Lightning Source LLC
Chambersburg PA
CBHW071120100726
47908CB00008B/2438